THE
BOOMER CREW

PETER SEDDON

The Boomer Crew

Published 2023

ISBN 9798393988111

Dedicated to John Henry Seddon.
Thank you for everything. I love you, Dad.
1948–2022

CHAPTER ONE

It felt like spring would never come. The sky over Glebe End had been ashen for days and warmth was hard to find. The streets were slick with ice, the cars thick with frost, but the cold was coldest at the Albemarle allotments. Far away from the traffic and the inner-city noise (which were omnipresent, even on Sundays), the allotments were calm. A blackbird hopped along the frost-tipped grass. A robin chirped. And, as a local tabby settled on his shed roof, Blake Campbell steered his wheelbarrow towards a raised soil bed.

His fingers were ice cold under his soil-stained gloves as he steered the old barrow away from the modest comfort of his tool shed, where he had left a cup of hot tea waiting for his return. Pushing and steering, he was daydreaming of the steaming bath he planned to have later when his allotment neighbour, Gottfried (better known as Geoff), appeared at the small gate that divided their narrow parcels of land.

'Morning, Blakey. What you working on?'

'Rhubarb.' Blakey set down his barrow. 'You know the secret to good rhubarb?'

Geoff shook his head.

Blakey wiped his gloves on his overalls. 'Well, that's what the barra's for, see? This time of year there's nothing better than a fresh layer of manure on your rhubarb.'

'Really? I normally just have custard with mine.'

Blakey picked up his barrow, feeling the weight of the manure in his knees. 'Here I am, giving growing tips to a bloke who pitches up every week in a shirt and tie. A shirt and tie!'

'What's that supposed to mean?' Geoff checked his attire.

'You don't grow much, do you, Geoff? Never have, never will. I don't know why you bother coming.'

Blakey pushed his barrow off as an ear-splitting sound erupted from Geoff's side of the fence. It was a creaking, grinding noise, and the ground vibrated as if they were standing at the epicentre of an earthquake. A shrill shriek of metal filled their ears and both men dropped to their knees and instinctively covered their heads.

'What the bloody hell is that?' Blakey said, trying to make sense of the catastrophic din.

A tall mast, not unlike a slimmed-down telephone tower, lurched and swayed near Geoff's shed. Blakey had seen the structure before, of course. It had been behind Geoff's shed for years and he had never questioned it, in the same way no one ever questioned Blakey's collection of nude garden gnomes. But the thing next to Geoff's shed had never swayed before; it usually stood stock still, like a nude gnome.

'For crying out loud, Geoff. It's bad enough you don't actually grow anything on your plot – not even a parsnip in five years, which, dare I say it, is denying other members of the community the joys of fresh herbs, potatoes, cucumbers, and possibly tomatoes – but now that thing you've got sticking up by your shed is falling down. What's it for anyway?'

Geoff winced at the lopsided tower. 'It's a vertical dipole antenna,' he said. 'It's part of a ham radio rig I use to keep in touch with my mother and brother back in Germany.'

'Your mum? Is that old bird still going? She must be over a hundred to have you as a son, cos you're no spring chicken, are you? You're so old, your first car must have been a covered wagon.'

'You're five years older than me.'

'But I'm young at heart, aren't I? And never mind this antenna; have you ever heard of that hot new invention called the telephone?'

Geoff sneered. 'Where's the fun with that?'

'Well, there isn't going to be much fun for either of us if that thing comes down on our heads. Aren't you going to fix it?'

Geoff adjusted his flat cap and squinted at the tall, listing antenna. 'Ah, I see. One of the steel support cables has come off. It needs four cables with equal tension on each side to keep it upright. So I tell you what – I'll steady the base while you go up top and reattach the cable.'

'Me? Go up there? You must be mad. Why don't you do it?'

'You know about my bad hip.'

'Don't I ever. All you talk about is your hip. And I can't go up there. It's about two storeys high and it doesn't look very safe, does it?'

'It's not two storeys high and there are footholds the length of the structure. Just think of it as a fun ladder.'

'Oh, real funhouse, that thing. I might die laughing, and falling, obviously. Can't you call someone to repair it?'

'Well … The equipment isn't exactly legal, in the strictest sense. Not that it can cause anyone any harm.'

'Harm? It's about to fall on our heads!'

'That's why you have to help. It's either that or, by the look of things, it's going to come down right on top of your rhubarb.'

'Hey, you leave my 'barb out of this.' Blakey felt a swell of annoyance. He'd rather disappear back to his shed, back to his strong cuppa and Radio 4, but how could he relax with that chunk of metal about to come crashing down on him? Neighbours, eh?

'Balls to it,' he said. 'Come on, show me what needs doing.'

CHAPTER TWO

The antenna rocked on its base, bobbed and weaved, and finally settled in a lopsided position, held in place by the remaining three cables.

'We'd better do it now before the wind picks up. I'm not sure how long the three other anchor points will hold,' Geoff said, as he ambled back to his shed. He ducked inside and came back out with a questionable-looking, paint-splattered ladder and set it up next to the listing antenna.

Blakey looked at the heady heights of the ladder's apex.

'Tall, isn't it?'

He put his hands on the ladder's frame and put one foot on the bottom rung, testing it for stability, all the while wondering why he had agreed to do this.

'Channel your inner Fred Dibnah,' Geoff said, giving him a thumbs up. 'And you'll need this.' He handed Blakey a long length of steel cable that had a reinforced loop at the end. 'It's the original support cable that came loose. The other end of it is staked into the ground over there.'

Blakey took a deep breath. 'Suppose Dibnah wasn't afraid of a ladder.' He stuck the loop in his back pocket and stepped on the second rung, the cable trailing behind him, flapping from his pocket like a tail. The ladder's feet sank a little into the ground, but it was steady, so he climbed to the top.

He could see over all the other sheds on the allotment, to every managed and mismanaged strip of fertile land, and even to the vehicles in the car park. The roof of Alan's motorhome needed a clean – the solar panel and the wind turbine were covered in dirt so he made a mental note to tell him when he was back on terra firma. A gentle breeze played with the remaining hair on his head as he looked down at Geoff.

'Exactly what am I supposed to do again?'

Geoff pointed further up the antenna. 'Put the eye of the steel cable on the hook midway up, then I can ratchet the tower upright.'

'That simple, eh? Well, I've got news for you – the ladder's not tall enough.'

'You'll have to climb up the antenna itself to get closer. It's only a few feet further, so use the footholds. And don't worry, the anchor points will probably hold the antenna in position for a while.'

'How long's a while?'

Geoff played deaf.

Sod it, Blakey thought. He'd come this far.

His first foot on the antenna took his weight but as soon as his other foot was on, the tower leaned back on the remaining three cables.

'Bugger me!' he yelped.

'What was that?' Geoff shouted.

'I said, bugger me!'

'Oh, just get on with it.'

The antenna became more animated with every movement, rocking slowly at first, then gathering pace and pivoting like a pendulum. It felt like the start of a carnival ride, the Wurlitzer or Teacups. He wasn't much for rides or rollercoasters but he had a job to do, so he took the steel loop from his pocket and reached up to the hook, having finally come within stretching distance. But his hand was an agonising inch away and his shoulder started to tire, so he put both hands back on the antenna's frame and drew breath.

'What the 'eck are you doing, Grandad?' came a yell from below. Blakey looked down. His nineteen-year-old grandson, Charlie, was fresh on the scene with his girlfriend, Robin. What on earth were they doing here? Charlie was supposed to be at training.

Then the wind picked up.

'I could see you up there all the way from the street,' Charlie hollered, 'so I had to come and see what you're up to.'

Charlie was sniggering, but that was the least of Blakey's worries. Glancing down from this new height, from this weird perspective, made him feel suddenly ill. The wind made it worse, like someone was turning up the speed on the Teacups-slash-Wurlitzer, and the more he tried to maintain equilibrium, the more the antenna danced and the more his stomach backflipped, until all he could do was cling on for dear life. All he had wanted to do was tend to some rhubarb. How had that become a life-threatening episode?

'Straight on TikTok, this,' Charlie yelled from below as he pointed his phone at Blakey.

Blakey tried to reach the hook again, and again his movement worsened the wonky equilibrium of his situation. But with one brave reach, the cable met the hook and oh, what a relief.

'Good,' Geoff shouted. 'Now come down and I'll pull the antenna upright.'

Finally! Time for that cuppa.

Blakey relaxed a little as he probed downward with his feet, looking for a lower rung, still asking himself why it was so hard to relax on Sundays. The swing and bounce of the structure made him second-guess every move and every redistribution of weight. He felt thankful it was almost over; his shoulder was already sore from all the stretching and reaching.

He glanced down to measure his next step, breathing heavily and noticing how stiff his fingers had become. His grip failed and he panicked and grabbed at the metal frame, but nothing seemed to slow down his descent, not even the lower rung that his foot was supposed to land on. He tried to hold on to something, anything, but he was already in free fall, tumbling towards earth with increasing speed, his scream echoing over the allotment. He braced for impact, feeling a dreadful weightlessness, knowing the landing was going to hurt. He prayed for no broken bones, he hoped he wouldn't die, but he tasted death in the air and his mind raced with visions: his beloved wife, Lizzie. Charlie's first football game. Glebe Town lifting the cup. He saw his retirement gifts from the boys in the workshop. He saw rhubarb. And ... Captain Fin.

CHAPTER THREE

A noise followed, a loud one, the sound of breaking, a collision at high speed. Then the falling stopped and all was quiet. Blakey opened his eyes, feeling like he'd just been shot out of a cannon, and saw that he was bathed in light from an opening in the sky. A portal.

'Can you hear me?' cried a voice.

'Is that you, Captain Fin?' Blakey blinked at the light.

'What?'

'Am I in heaven?'

'No, you're not.'

'Oh no, you mean … I'm down there. What did I do to deserve this?'

'You broke my shed roof, that's what you did. Now get up, fatso.'

Blakey looked about, rubbed his face and struggled to focus. Geoff was there. And Charlie too, leaning on his girlfriend, sobbing. No, giggling. And staring at his phone, as usual.

'Wow, 3k views on TikTok already!' Charlie said, mid-guffaw.

'What the bloody hell happened?' Blakey said. 'Where am I?'

'Well, you didn't really fall, in the classic sense,' Geoff said. 'You kind of rode the antenna down, and ended up crashing through my shed roof and splashing down on my sofa.'

'You've got a sofa in yer shed?' The interior was unusual for an allotment shed, Blakey could see that. There were no tools or bags of compost or used plant pots, not even a trowel. It was clean, warm, comfortable, and filled with silver-coloured electronic equipment, like the middle spread of a 1980s hi-fi catalogue.

'Yeah, I got a sofa, a broken one, thanks to you,' Geoff said.

'Look.' Charlie showed his mobile to Blakey. Tom Petty's song 'Free Fallin' filled the speakers, while a shaky video of Blakey's downfall played. The footage showed him plummeting through Geoff's roof, then popping up the antenna again, like toast springing from a toaster.

Blakey checked the portal above him and saw it was just a jagged hole in the roof, with sharp points of torn wood sticking out in all directions. The antenna stood above it, pointing up at the sky. This was all somewhat anticlimactic, but a relief.

'I thought that was it,' Blakey said. 'I thought my number had come up, and all I get from my grandson is mockery. I might have died.'

Charlie giggled. 'Dibs on your car.'

'You don't know you're born, you, lad. And that car's going to your dad.'

'Calm down, Grandad. You didn't fall that far.'

Blakey rolled his eyes. When did Charlie stop taking life seriously? Blakey supposed there was nothing wrong with a rum sense of humour, but Charlie definitely got it from his mother.

Blakey sat up. 'Wait a sec. Why aren't you at football training? They'll release you if you play truant.'

The smile disappeared from Charlie's face. 'Let's not get into this now.'

'Into what? If you play your cards right you'll get a run in the cup.'

'No chance. I hardly get a game and now they've told me I have to train with the reserves midweek. The coach says I've not shown enough progress.' Charlie pulled a face. 'I think they're going to terminate my contract at the end of the season. Ah, leave it, you've spoilt the mood now.'

Robin knelt in front of Blakey, her auburn hair cresting at her shoulders. 'Are you okay, Mr Campbell? It's a good job the couch was here to break your fall.'

'I'm alright, lass, thanks.'

'And never mind the roof,' Geoff said. 'I'm sure you'll find time to fix it.'

'Buggered if I will,' Blakey said. 'Just call it a skylight and have done with it.'

'Who's Captain Fin?' Robin asked. 'You mentioned that name.'

'Cap Fin? Oh yeah, that's my old mate from school. He was absolutely it. The coolest lad you ever met. Even the teachers loved him – they wouldn't tell him off for smoking in the bike shed or anything. It's funny the things that go through your head when you have a shock.'

'Was he your captain in the army, like in World War Two?' Robin said.

'Eee, I'm not that old, love. No, he wasn't in the army or anything like that. He was captain of the school football team, and everyone that watched him said he was the next Wilf McGuinness. Had scouts from Preston North End come and watch him and everything. But after school, he took a job down the pit and did his knee in, and that was his playing days over. I lost touch with him years ago but I tell you what, he could show Charlie a thing or two when it comes to football.'

'Sounds like a right one,' Robin said. 'And you're sure you're okay?'

'You're a good 'un, you, love. I'm okay.' He gestured to Charlie. 'But do me a favour and tell him to stop staring at his phone.'

'Blimey, over 5k views now,' Charlie said. 'You're trending, Grandad.'

'Always been trendy, me, pal.'

Robin smiled. 'How about I take you to the Walk-In Centre for a check-over? A man of your age, falling like that.'

Blakey stood up and stretched.

'Everything seems to be in order, but I'll not lie, I thought I was a goner. I thought I was at the pearly gates, but I appear to be in my usual tip-top condition. In fact, I feel a bit better than normal, like a fog has been lifted. Everything seems clearer, simpler. It's like I've been shaken up and given a reminder that life's for living. A second chance. It's funny how a near-death experience revitalises you.'

'Near-death?' Geoff said. 'You're seventy-four. You're always near death.'

'Well, I feel like I could take on the world right now. Come on, Geoff. We've sat in our sheds decomposing like compost for too long. We should be out there, doing whatever we want, like when we were young. Let's go to a rock concert or go wild camping or fishing. The world's our oyster.'

'I can't go anywhere,' Geoff protested. 'I've a dentist appointment in the morning.'

'Come on. Old is just a state of mind. Let's live a little.'

'That's the spirit,' Robin said. 'But you sure you're not just concussed?'

'By 'eckers, like.'

Robin narrowed her eyes.

'Forget it,' Blakey muttered. As ever, people had other things to do. Same old story, and he knew his grandson would be no different, but he wasn't about to let that stop him. 'If no one wants to get out there with me and have some fun, I'll just have to track down my old mate, Cap Fin … Now there's an idea …' When they were teenagers, Cap Fin was always his go-to partner in crime. 'It's about time I paid him a visit. Although, I've no idea where he's living now.' Blakey scanned his memory. 'Got no number for him either.' Still, he wasn't getting any younger and if he wanted to find his old mate, now was the time to start searching. 'Right, no time like the present,' he said. 'I'm off to find my old pal.'

'Charlie,' Robin said, in a tone that sounded like a command rather than a namecheck.

'What?' Charlie moaned.

Robin eyed her boyfriend.

'Okay,' Charlie said. 'How about this, Geoff – I'll fix the roof if you make sure my grandad doesn't keel over while he goes looking for his friend. I'd watch him myself, but I'm waiting for a call from the *Glebe Observer*. They've just replied to my TikTok video and said they want to come and interview me about what happened to Grandad. Local interest piece, they said.'

Geoff winced. 'As much as I'd love to help your grandad, I've got a hotpot in the slow cooker. I'm sure Blakey understands. Blakey … Blakey? Where's he gone?'

They peered out of the shed door. Blakey was striding across the allotment. Charlie smiled.

'Er, Geoff. You'd better get a wriggle on if you want that roof fixing.'

CHAPTER FOUR

Blakey spotted Geoff giving chase behind him, yelling and waving. With no loss of purpose, Blakey marched through the gate to his lot, towards the sanctuary of his own shed. He shimmied around the wheelbarrow, hopped over the puddle, threw open the shed door and finally got his hands on that cup of tea he'd left waiting. He took a mouthful, ice cold though it was, and removed his car keys from the hook and headed for the door.

Geoff stopped him at the entrance.

'I said, where are you going?' He blew out his cheeks, visibly exhausted after a sprint.

'Like I said, I'm going to find my old pal. Fin knew how to enjoy himself. I bet he doesn't have one foot in the grave like you.'

Geoff leaned on the door frame. 'You really shouldn't drive after a fall like that. It's best you get checked over, just to be sure.'

Blakey tossed Geoff the keys to his mustard-yellow, lovingly restored, chromed-to-the-teeth 1978 Mk2 Ford Escort. 'Fine, you drive. But don't scratch my car. That thing is priceless.'

Geoff juggled the keys, struggling to get a grip of the jingle-jangling bunch of 'World's Best Grandad' keyrings. 'The only place I'll be driving you is the Walk-In Centre,' he said.

Blakey ran his fingers through his hair, trying to decide how best to explain it to Geoff. 'Look, I've been thinking ...'

'Oh dear,' Geoff said.

'No no, don't be like that. Listen, I've been thinking ... reminiscing, I suppose, about the old days, about old friends and people I used to know ... and I've realised that I've lost touch with everyone from my youth.'

'So?'

Blakey felt flustered; he could feel his cheeks getting red. He wrung his hands and said it as best he could. 'Haven't you ever lost touch with someone you were close to and regretted it? You must have. You can't be as old as we are without drifting apart from someone ... and isn't it a shame when that happens?'

'It happens to everyone at some point,' Geoff said, mopping his brow with a handkerchief. 'That's life.'

'It's not the life I want. So, listen here, I'm not afraid to say it if I have to.'

'Say what?'

Blakey waved him off and reached for his tea mug. 'You know ...'

'Sorry, I don't—'

Blakey threw his enamelled mug at the wall and tea sprayed all over his radio, his tools and spare overalls. The cup clattered across the floor and came to a halt.

'I'm not afraid to say that I miss my mate, okay?'
Blakey lowered himself into a plastic lawn chair.
'Sorry, Geoff. It's just taken me about forty years to
find the courage to admit it. Maybe it's my age, but it
really breaks my heart to know that I'm a stranger to
the people I used to call friends … the ones that are
still around, anyway.' Blakey felt hot and bothered.
'You know, back when I was a kid, me and Fin spent
the best days of our youth together, side by side. I
miss that friendship.'

Geoff took off his flat cap and squeezed it as he
looked at the tea-stained floor. 'You've never
mentioned this before.'

'It's hardly allotment banter, is it?' Blakey shook
his head at the mess he'd made. 'I didn't think much
of it at first, but over time it's sneaked into my
thoughts here and there. Then more as time went on,
until I realised that I've got this dull pain inside. It's
taken me a while to figure out what it is, but I know
now. Remembering Fin has made me realise I'm
lonely, Geoff … I'm bloody lonely. And the fact that
I can't pick up the phone and chat with the friend that
I was closest to pains me. Sure, I have family and
mates, but no friends.'

'If he was such a good pal, how come you lost
touch?'

Blakey shrugged. 'We got older and drifted apart,
what with life, kids, grandkids, work. Everything got

in the way. And I got lazy, too. Thought we'd be in touch at some point. But the years fly by, don't they?'

Geoff shuffled at the door. 'How can you be sure he's even still alive?'

'Oh, he's alive. I guarantee it. No stopping Cap Fin. Plus ... I keep an eye on the obituaries. Seen a few of my old school mates in there. Most of my friends, truth be told. I was sad to read Benny had gone. Cancer. And Murph went the same way. Good lads, they were. But there's never been any mention of any Finley John.' Blakey picked his mug up from the floor and started wiping tea off the walls.

Geoff shook his head. 'If it means this much to you, I'll help you find him.'

Blakey felt a blush of optimism. 'You can start by showing me a copy of the phone book.'

'Now you're really showing your age,' Geoff said. 'Phone books have gone the way of Woolworths.'

'Well, how the bloody hell do you find anyone nowadays?'

Geoff shrugged. 'The internet?'

'Is anyone our age on that? Do you own a computer?'

Geoff shook his head.

Blakey's enthusiasm wavered. All he had was an old mobile phone, one with real buttons and no internet. Perhaps it was all for the best, he thought. The inclination to reach out after all these years was probably just an episode that's best forgotten.

Embarrassing, maybe, and Geoff might be right: perhaps this is just how it was supposed to be, the way things were as you got older. But when was Geoff ever right?

Blakey was in a muddle as he cleaned the last of the splattered tea.

Charlie's voice rattled across the allotment, his voice panicked, desperate.

'Grandad, Grandad! Come quick!'

CHAPTER FIVE

What had become of the morning? Sundays were not what they used to be. Blakey had never run so much on a day of rest. Another hop over the puddle, a shimmy around the wheelbarrow and back through the gate. By the time he glanced at the still unmanured rhubarb, he was out of breath and back at Geoff's shed.

'Charlie-Boy, you okay?' He could hardly talk for panting.

Charlie was inside, smiling, phone still in hand. 'I'm alright, but you look like you're about to burst.'

'You scared me half to death, whimpering like that. What's all the fuss?'

He needn't have asked. A woman holding a large camera and a furry microphone was sitting by Robin on Geoff's rumpled couch.

'You must be the superstar grandad,' she said, beaming.

'And to whom do I owe the pleasure?' Blakey took off his muddy gloves and patted down the creases in his overalls.

She stood up and extended a hand. 'Rachael Ribbons.' Her smile was wide and her brown eyes twinkled with excitement, although she looked a little out of place on the allotment thanks to her tailored grey suit, bright-blue blouse and slicked-back hair. 'I'm with the *Glebe Observer*,' she said. 'Did Charlie mention that I was popping over to do a piece for the online edition? We have to be fast when something local starts getting attention like this. Now, if we could have a quick chat on camera, that would be grand.'

Blakey stepped forward. 'Online edition? Wait … is that on the internet?'

'Exactly.' Rachael started setting up her camera. 'I'll upload the video as soon as I get back to the office. We have to be right up to the minute with the news these days: it's the only way to compete with social media.'

'Oh, I say.' Blakey straightened the collar of his shabby overalls. 'So, I'll talk into that camera and that'll go on the internet?' he said, working it all out.

But Rachael was too busy clipping a small microphone between the buttons on his overalls to listen. She checked the camera's screen, repositioned him to get the best light and pointed the lens at him. 'So, how does it feel to be an internet sensation?'

'Last time I was a sensation it was 1967 and I was busting a move on the dancefloor at the Twisted Wheel. Those Motown tunes always got my hips going.' He wiggled his bum. 'Good exercise, it was. But never mind that.' Blakey looked into the camera. 'Listen, er, internet, I'm after catching up with an old pal. I lost touch with him, and people say you can find folk on the internet. Well, I don't own a computer, so if anyone knows where Finley John is these days, come and see me. He's in his seventies, a bit taller than me, and he had a belting left foot. You can find me at my allotment, or you can ask at the Dog and Duck or—'

'I'm not sure that's the kind of thing the newspaper is after,' Charlie said.

'No, it's perfect,' Rachael said. 'What a heart-warming story! Oh, imagine the clicks this'll get. Friends Reunited, eat your heart out.' She retrieved the microphone, whipped out a notepad and led Charlie out of the shed, saying, 'Now, let me make sure I've got all your details …'

Blakey watched her walk off. 'Suppose that's that,' he said. 'What a day.'

'She didn't even ask about my shed,' Geoff said. 'Good job too.' He bounced his eyebrows. 'I don't want the authorities finding out about my gear.'

'It all looks very high-tech in here,' said Robin, 'or low-tech, depending on how you look at it.'

'Will the gear be okay?' Blakey said, looking at the hole in the roof and at the amplifiers, microphones and other equipment he couldn't identify.

'Yeah. Nothing a tarp can't cover till the roof is sorted.'

'Sorry I smashed your shed.'

'Be fine. I can still scan the airwaves and talk to my old radio buddies, or maybe find new ones. Dying breed we are these days, radio enthusiasts. Sometimes I wonder if I'll track down an old friend – from real life, I mean; people I've met way back when – on the off chance they picked up the radio habit at some point. But truth be told, some days all I get is static.' Geoff started covering the radio gear with a rain cover. Blakey picked up a corner of the tarp and helped drape it over the desk full of equipment.

'How long have you been in England now?' Blakey said, wondering why he'd never asked that question before.

'Going on forty years. All my childhood friends are about a thousand miles that way.' Geoff gestured to the distance with a handful of tarp. 'I have plenty of people from the home country that I speak to on the phone from time to time, but I prefer the radio. It's much more fun. So, I scan and scan, mostly hoping to bump into someone special.'

Robin raised an eyebrow. 'Special?'

Geoff's eyes twinkled. 'Lina, her name was. My first love. She used to be into radio, but I think she just used to say that because I was into it. Believe it or not, back then I liked to tinker with the latest tech. Yeah … me and her had a good time for a while, until we broke up. And that was that.'

'Ah, the age-old story,' Blakey mused.

'Yeah. I wanted her but she didn't want me. Then she moved to another city to study and we never saw each other again. Which means the last time we spoke, I was a teenager, and that'll be the last memory she has of me. It's a shame, really, because so much time has passed, we'd be completely different people now. I've moved to England and been married and divorced since her, but I'd still love to talk to her one last time just to see how it all worked out. It's funny; we were the main characters in each other's lives for a while there, but now we'll never know how it turned out in the end. So yeah, I do know what it's like to lose someone – not to death but to circumstances – so I hope you find your old pal. And if I can help, I will.'

CHAPTER SIX

The row of benches outside the Dog and Duck were full of men in red football shirts laughing and talking over their pints as Blakey walked by.

Fifty years, he thought as he walked inside the pub. That's how long he'd been coming to the Dog and Duck; not religiously, but often enough. His proper local had been the Gardener's Arms, but they'd turned it into flats. The Dog and Duck was close to the allotments, which was handy, and it reminded him of the old days since there'd been only one major refurb in all that time.

The front door was an original feature, imposing and dark, with heavy bolts on the inside. There were still old taxi service business cards pinned to the back of it too, most of which were long out of business. If you called those numbers now, who knew who would answer? The benches in the beer garden and the TVs on the walls were all new, but the old hand-cut ceiling beams were still on show inside, although they didn't stand out as much now because they'd been painted pale grey. The old cast-iron fireplace was where it always had been, but instead of a fire in its middle there was a pile of dusty logs, which Blakey had always assumed were purely decorative because he'd not seen the fire lit in this place for decades. Such a waste. The place still did a decent pint of mild, though, even if the pump had been moved to the far end to make way for the modern beer pumps; there was a massive new one that was covered in chrome and ice, another one had some sort of liquid whirlwind spinning in a glass orb at its top, and the one next to it glowed red and pulsed like a heartbeat. There were lots of fancy Spanish beers too, all of which tasted the same to Blakey, not that he minded Spain.

'Pint of mild, please, Al,' Blakey said as he approached the bar.

With a nod, bald Al worked the pump with his trademark aggressive style, his white shirt rolled up to his elbows, revealing an array of tattoos. 'Bit early for you, isn't it? Don't usually see you in here till after the match,' he said above the chatter and the TV.

'Been a right morning. Thought I could use an early one.'

Al sat a glistening amber pint on the bar. 'How's your grandson these days?'

'Thick as rhubarb.'

'It's the semi-final of the Lancashire FA Challenge Cup soon, you know. You think he'll make the team?'

'It doesn't seem like it, no. So don't go putting any money on him scoring the winner.'

Blakey paid and turned to the TV, where talking heads were hyping up the local Premier League derby. He sighed. He could only dream of watching Charlie play for one of the big clubs, the kind that got on TV. What the bloody hell would that young thicko do if he lost his contract? He wasn't fit for owt.

'This you?' Al held his phone over the bar, his face creasing into a smile. 'Didn't know you were a celeb.'

It was the *Glebe Observer* article, hot off the press, accompanied by a video of Blakey talking to the camera.

'News travels fast these days, I see. I'm after my old pal, Finley John – that's what I'm on about there.'

Al scratched his head. 'Finley John? I know a bloke by that name; he used to come in here regular.'

Blakey choked on his mild. 'I've never seen him in here!'

'He never makes an appearance on weekends, or on a match day. In fact, I've not seen him for a while. He used to hang out at the park, I think, feeding the birds and all that before he'd pop in for a morning half. He'd usually be outside waiting for the pub to open with a copy of the *Metro* under his arm. He always drank a half, never more than that. And he'd make it last.'

'Well I never. What park you on about?'

'Dewsbury.'

Blakey couldn't believe Cap Fin had been frequenting the same pub as him, at some point anyway. He sipped his pint and pondered a trip to the park.

Geoff walked in. 'Figured you'd be here,' he said. 'I've still got your car keys and this is the only place in walking distance from the allotment. You're quick on your feet when you want to be. I hadn't noticed you dash off after Charlie started talking about repairing the roof.'

'Sorry, mate. I just fancied a pint on my own.'

Geoff sat on a bar stool. 'No wonder you've got no friends. I thought you might appreciate some company. And like I said, I'll help find your friend if you like.'

'On that note – you'll never believe this – turns out I have a lead, thanks to Al. You fancy a trip to the park?'

'On match day? It'll be carnage down there.'

'Give over. Just get a pint down you and let's go.'

Blakey and Geoff walked along the gravel path, through the wrought-iron gates and into Dewsbury Park, a little common of grassy open land frequented by joggers and dog walkers in the mornings, and youths with no better place to go in the evenings. Except on weekends. On weekends it was taken over by away footy fans, and this weekend's guests were the most dreaded fans of all: local rivals, Coltan Rangers.

The park was full of the ballyhoo of match day. Fans gathered around benches and loitered at the war memorial. Joshing and public drinking seemed to be the main occupation of the pre-match hoard, for most of them anyway. From a distance, Blakey spotted one shirtless young man making a noise and puffing out his chest, goading another man who was sitting in front of him on the concrete steps of the monument. Typical behaviour for derby day.

'Look at the state of these,' Geoff said. 'And him over there with his chest out.'

'It's already turned sour,' Blakey said.

'I'm not sure we should be here,' Geoff muttered.

The youth could be heard shouting, 'You old git! Look at you, you're pathetic,' as he stood over a frail-looking figure with a newspaper under his arm.

'Bloody hooligan.' Blakey's blood began to boil and he couldn't help but take a closer look.

'I don't think you should be going too close,' Geoff said.

'Don't worry. If he turns on me, I'll give him a thick ear.'

Before Blakey could get close, the angry man swung a furious right hand. The old man in front of him couldn't react quickly enough, and the thwacking sound suggested contact was perfect. The older man leaned to one side and absorbed the shock of the assault.

A follow-up left hand landed clean while the other fans stood about and pretended not to notice. After another blow, the victim buckled under a flurry of follow-up punches and put up his hands and finally cried out for mercy, trying to stop the attack. The surrounding football fans turned away.

Blakey gritted his teeth. 'Oi! Get off him, you yob!' The old man looked defeated and sorrowful. He also looked familiar. He looked like Cap Fin, but older. Like an aged Gary Oldman with stubble. Could it really be him?

Blakey turned to the youth.

'You think you're tough, picking on an old man while he's sat down trying to enjoy the park?'

The young man squared up to Blakey, nose to nose. His breath reeked of whisky.

'This is my park, Grandad.'

'Since when?'

'Since I said so.' A flame flickered in the man's eyes and he pulled back a fist.

CHAPTER SEVEN

At the age of seventy-four, it's fair to say that Blakey had lost a step (okay, several steps), but when required, he could get as angry as any youth. He smacked the hooligan in the jaw and dropped him to a knee. But the man sprang to his feet and looked angrier than ever. Blakey glanced at Geoff, hoping for a little backup, but Geoff had taken a few steps away.

The yob rubbed his chin and shook his head as if his rage was going supernova.

'You're going to pay for that.'

He raised his hands like a boxer warming up a jab and swung for Blakey.

Charlie sprinted into view and hit the yob with a ferocious rugby tackle. The two of them crashed to the floor in a tangled heap, but Charlie got the advantage and pummelled the yob with a series of punches, UFC style. And with one last punch to satisfy himself, Charlie got up and let the lad slink away.

'Now piss off,' Charlie roared.

The surrounding fans suddenly acknowledged what was going on and let out an ironic cheer in the direction of the youth as he retreated.

'You okay, Grandad?' Charlie said, face flushed, out of breath.

'You come in useful sometimes, you do. And I'm alright, thanks, Charlie.'

Charlie took a breath and shook his head. 'I was coming to tell you about the ton of Facebook messages I received about your mate. What was his name? John Finley?'

'Finley John.'

'Him too. Al told me you were headed here so I thought I better come find you. This park is a ghetto.'

'It's not this bad most days,' Blakey said. 'Besides, I heard my mate might be here and, believe it or not, he is.'

'Where?'

'Right there.' Blakey turned to where the man was sitting, or rather *had* been sitting.

Blakey asked Geoff, 'Did you see where he went?'

Geoff pointed up the gravel path. 'Out through the park gates.'

'Bugger me.' Blakey couldn't believe his luck. So close, yet so far. He could see Cap Fin ambling across the busy road beyond the park. Cars and buses were whizzing either side of him so close that the number 163 bus had to slam on the brakes to avoid hitting him. A car coming the other way swerved around Fin as he continued crossing. Horns blared, tyres screeched, and a chorus of angry shouts could be heard from red faces behind windscreens.

'Wait!' Blakey walked briskly towards the road. His heart was racing after the altercation and running wasn't on the cards: he'd done too much today already. Waiting for the traffic lights to turn green, he watched Cap Fin disappear into the churchyard as the twelve o'clock church bells chimed.

Geoff and Charlie joined Blakey as the red man finally turned green, and they quickstepped across the tarmac. Blakey hollered after his long-lost friend and followed him into the churchyard, where the noise of the cars faded to a semi-distant, calming whoosh.

Among the flowers and the tombstones, Cap Fin stood in the far corner, wiping his eyes.

It was definitely him.

Blakey composed himself. 'Stay here,' he whispered to Charlie and Geoff. Feeling nervous, he quietly approached.

His old pal … so old now.

'You okay, mate? I've been looking for you. Why'd you run off?'

Cap Fin fixed his eyes on a small tombstone adorned with yesterday's flowers: posies, like the ones that grew in the park. The headstone read: *Ella John. We Will Always Love You. 1948–2013*.

'Ah. Ella. She was a wonderful lady, Cap.'

Fin snorted. 'Don't call me Cap. No one's called me Cap for fifty years. The name's Finley.' He was dishevelled, wrapped up in a long, worn-out navy-blue overcoat. His beard was fuzzy, his hair messy, and his left eye was already starting to bruise from the incident in the park. The wrinkles around Finley's eyes surprised Blakey, having held in his mind the image of a fresh-faced young man for all these years.

'There she is … lovely Ella,' Finley said.

Blakey nodded.

'Been ten years now. I come here most days to tend to her. She's always here waiting for me, even though I really wish she was at home, drinking her sherry and watching her soaps.' His voice cracked. He cleared his throat. 'Blakey, isn't it? It's been a while.'

'Aye.'

'Well, here's something they never taught us when we were young: you get old and you die, and that's all there is to it.'

'Give over. You can't do much about dying,' Blakey said. 'We can just live for today. You know how it is.'

Finley sighed. 'I know all too well how it is. And I know how it used to be, too. You remember when we were kids. When the old people seemed really old, Victorian really. They all had crinkly faces and old-fashioned clothes. And they had proper ways and means about them – airs and graces, I mean. And they had family to see them off when the time came.'

Blakey let the silence breathe, not sure what to say.

Finley continued. 'I remember being at my grandma's house when she died. I was by her bedside; the whole family was. And it was the same when my grandfather went a few years later. I remember looking at him and those great big hands … I never realised I'd get that old. And now I'm his age and our generation seems doomed to die in an old folks' home. And death's around the corner, I can feel it coming on, but we're not supposed to talk about it, are we? People look at you like they're suddenly late for an appointment when you bring it up, that's if you can stop them staring at their phone.'

'Come on, Finley. There's plenty of life left in us yet.'

Finley shook his head. 'You have to say that. Everybody says that, but it's not true.'

'You might have another twenty or thirty years in you for all you know.'

'Thirty years of what, exactly? Heartbreak? Deterioration? Not for me, thanks. It only gets worse from here.'

'I tell you what, why don't I walk you home and see to your black eye? Then we'll get a sherry and toast to Ella. Where you living now?'

Finley pulled out a handkerchief and wiped his nose.

'You do have a place to stay, don't you?' Blakey said.

'Course I have,' Finley snapped.

'Well, what do you say, then? Should we get back there?'

Finley turned away. 'Fine. You can walk me back to mine, but you can't come in.'

'Why not?'

'Because you wouldn't like what you'd find.'

CHAPTER EIGHT

Finley winced with every step. Blakey and Geoff followed alongside. Blakey had sent Charlie on his way but Geoff insisted on helping, possibly fearing that his new acquaintance might be too fragile to make it home. Blakey was worried too; next to Finley's slow, withered figure, he felt positively spritely.

'You ever had kids, Finley?' Geoff asked.

'Yeah, and grandkids.'

'See them much?' Blakey said.

Finley shook his head. 'They've all got jobs and whatnot. Life keeps them busy.'

Blakey wondered what life would be like if Charlie didn't pop around as often as he did, and if Max, Blakey's son and Charlie's dad, didn't swing by once a week for a brew and a chat. He suddenly felt lucky for the visits he took for granted and it brought on a sense of melancholy.

They walked off the main road and rounded a corner into an estate full of two-storey apartment buildings. A sign by the gate said 'McLaren Court Sheltered Accommodation'. They followed Finley through the gates, down a narrow path, and headed towards the furthest block. They passed a small garden, which was a mere slip of grass with a bird feeder stuck in a tree stump. Finley got out his keys and approached a heavy-looking security door overlooking the stump.

'This is me,' Finley said, wiping his brow. 'Thanks for the walk, but you needn't have bothered. Cheerio.' As he readied his keys, they slipped from his hand and hit the floor. Bending down to pick them up, he froze and gasped for air. Blakey saw a reluctant plea in his eyes.

'I got you.' Blakey picked the keys up and walked Finley inside. Geoff took Finley's other shoulder and they guided him down a corridor.

'Number 22, just a little further down,' Finley whispered. 'I'll be alright once I've sat down. Just don't judge me, okay?'

Blakey tried to open the door to number 22 but it got stuck halfway. As he heaved it open, he heard things clatter to the ground on the other side but didn't think much about it. He was too preoccupied with navigating Finley across the room to a vinyl-covered armchair, the dry-wipeable kind. He saw something stir in Geoff's eyes but he couldn't figure out what it was until he looked around the dark interior of the flat.

The flat was tiny, no bigger than Blakey's garage, and made to feel all the smaller by the clutter that covered every surface. From the living room, Blakey could see through to the bathroom; the door was propped open by a heap of clothes, presumably unwashed. The kitchen was next door to it, with a sink full of empty Pot Noodle cups and a counter full of unwashed forks, spoons and tea towels. Behind the flat's front door, a broken vacuum cleaner, a selection of walking sticks and a set of crutches were piled. There was a broken TV across the two-seater couch in the living room. Newspapers and stacks of unopened letters were spewed over the coffee table, and the carpet was so dirty and so littered with shoes, ties, and old cans of Carlsberg that the only clear stretch of floor was the path from the door to Finley's armchair.

Blakey couldn't take it all in. What had become of his friend? Tension wrapped his chest. He felt angry.

'How the hell can you live like this!'

Finley shrank into his armchair and sighed. 'Sometimes, I don't know how I live at all.'

CHAPTER NINE

Blakey opened the curtains. A shaft of harsh light burst across the room. On the other side of the window the empty bird feeder teetered on the tree stump.

'How the mighty have fallen, eh?' Finley croaked. 'Used to be a beautiful blossom tree out there till the management had it chopped down. Bloody barbarians …'

The room looked even worse in the light of day. Dust swirled in the air above the carpet, and the stains were more on show.

Geoff looked about and attempted to smile. 'Nothing a bit of elbow grease can't fix.'

Blakey shook his head. He felt so disappointed.

'I know what you're thinking but it wasn't always like this,' Finley said. 'I guess I just lost control after Ella passed, and I kept telling myself I'd get on top of it, but it got worse and worse.'

'You can't live like this,' Blakey mumbled, regretting his anger at the situation. 'I'll help you put it right.'

'I'll help too,' Geoff said.

'What's the point?' Finley said. 'You know, I've spent a lot of time thinking recently, and I've realised there's a real dignity in just giving up.'

Blakey kneeled at Finley's chair. 'Come on, now. You've got to pull yourself together. Where's the flashy, charismatic lad I used to know?'

'He got old. Everyone just sees me as an old fart these days. I tried to stay positive, don't think I didn't try. But I never really asked for help because I didn't know you could.'

Blakey scanned the room, eyeing up the size of the problem. He noticed the coffee table again, overloaded with copies of the *Metro* newspaper, junk mail and serious-looking letters. 'What are these?' He gestured to what looked like bills, many of them unopened and marked 'Urgent'.

'Demands. Final ones.' Finley sighed. 'Gave up paying during Covid. Couldn't pay. My pension barely covers my rent and a few beers these days.'

'Well, we can reach out to whoever you owe money to and set up a payment plan,' Geoff said.

'Too late for that. I've been cut off. Now the council tax, the credit card and the overdraft are after me.'

'How much are you in a hole for?' Geoff asked.

'Dunno. Three, maybe four grand.'

Geoff puffed out his cheeks and leaned against the door frame.

'The only thing I've been able to keep up to date with is the rent on this place, and it's not cheap, you know, despite how it looks.' Finley shook his head. 'I kept telling myself it'd be alright next week. Then next week became next month and there was always too much month left at the end of the money and I kept thinking … it'll be alright next year; I'll get back on my feet … only I never did.'

Blakey was still finding it difficult to take in the situation and remain calm. 'This is no good. We're going to sort out your flat then sort out your money. We're going to get you back on your feet.'

'Bollocks,' Finley said, finding some energy. 'Just piss off and leave me alone. This is why I didn't want you coming in here.'

Blakey stood over him. 'I'm going nowhere till the bloke I once knew comes back. He's in there, he must be. And I get how you feel: I get fed up too. We all do. But you can't just throw in the towel.'

'Why don't you get out and meet some new people?' Geoff said. 'You'll feel better once you've got out of the house and done a bit of socialising. It'll change your perspective. Then maybe we can call up the credit card and the others to see what can be done.'

'Socialising? What for? I'm seventy-four.'

'It's never too late,' Geoff said. 'There's a club at the local retirement village near me; they put up bulletins in the town. Apparently, they meet every Thursday and solve murders – you know, crimes – all in the name of fun. You should go. There's a few lasses our age there, too, apparently.'

Finley pulled a face. 'Sounds like a bunch of do-gooders to me.'

'Let's sort the debt situation out first,' Blakey said, perching himself next to the broken television on the two-seater. 'I'll call the credit card company now if you like.'

Finley waved him away. 'I can't pay anything. I've no money or anything of value.'

'Then you're going to end up going to court,' Blakey cried. 'They can send you to jail for not paying your council tax, you know. And you can't do porridge at your age.'

Finley sneered. 'All that's going to sort me out right now is a wallop of cash,' he said. 'That's the only solution. Cash is the only thing these people understand. They're ruthless … I did talk to one of them once, and they basically told me to go get a credit card or they'd send the heavies round. Can you believe that?' He balled his fists. 'Trust me, I've tried everything to get on my feet but they don't want to help. They just want to bleed as much money out of me as they can. I even tried to start a business about seven years ago for some extra money. All I needed was the start-up capital. Money, standing in my way again … Anyway, I put together a business plan and went to that mangy bank manager, Derek Onions, you'll remember him – he was in our school, a few years below us. One time I had to give him a thick ear cos he told Ella that I'd kissed another lass when I hadn't.'

'Now you mention it, Derek Onions, yeah. I do remember him,' Blakey said. 'I always thought he was one of them compulsive liar types. I'm surprised he's made it to bank manager with the way he was. You know his dad was a plumber, right? Well, he once told me that Britain landed on the moon before the Americans did and his dad did the plumbing on the rocket. Reckoned his dad used the toilet just before launch.'

'Rockets don't have toilets,' Geoff said. 'The astronauts go in their suits.'

'Anyway,' Finley said, 'Derek's a bank manager now, if you can believe that, and he laughed off my loan application. Said I was too old to start a venture – he's almost my age! It was a good business idea, too.'

'Hope it wasn't a TV repair business,' Blakey said, looking at the knackered telly.

'It was a laundry business, smart-arse. And I had the machines and the premises and even the clients all lined up; the Indian restaurant on King's Street, the Chinese buffet down by the markets, and Al at the pub were all going to send me their tablecloths, napkins and towels. Had all that in writing. It would have been a good little earner, but that prick Derek turned me down flat for no good reason. Solid business plan, it was. He's my age and he's still working, so why can't I have another go around?' Finley reached into a Carlsberg box and pulled out a can. 'Short of robbing a bank there's nowt that can be done ... Now that's an idea … if Derek won't lend me the money, I should just take it. Cos if it's prison I'm going to, I might as well have some fun with it.' He smiled. 'If you want to help so much, how's about this … How about you help me rob a bank?' He chuckled and cracked open the can.

'This is no time for jokes,' Blakey said. 'Or drinking.'

'And why not?' Geoff said.

Blakey turned to him, astonished. 'What?'

'I mean, you said it yourself, you want a bit more adventure in your life,' Geoff said.

'Don't be ridiculous, I meant going camping or something——'

'Be a bit more fun than camping, I reckon,' Finley said, the old twinkle back in his eye. 'You want the old Fin back; that's what he'd do. Remember when we sneaked those Mars bars out of the school tuck shop?'

'Robbing a bank is a bit more than nicking a Mars bar, isn't it?' Blakey said.

'Definitely,' Finley said. Another youthful flush came over him and the smiling prankster from fifty years ago reappeared for the first time. 'Come on, you old sod. We can either laugh or cry, so let's have a laugh.'

CHAPTER TEN

'I don't believe what I'm hearing,' Blakey said. 'How exactly do three pensioners go about robbing a bank?'

'The same as anyone else,' Geoff said. 'Only slower.'

'I'm surprised at you,' Blakey said, shuffling around on the couch to face Geoff. 'Won't this interfere with your dentist appointment, or your hotpot? It'll be one overcooked hotpot if you have to do a stint in jail, won't it?'

Geoff screwed his face. 'You think I'm not bored? You think I like staying home all day, worrying about the dentist, all the while having the news tell me all the reasons I should be terrified: sunstroke on hot days, freezing to death on cold days, phone scammers, Covid, the Super Flu, Brexit, the cost of living, knife crime, gun crime, drug crime, random crime, thrill killers, the war in Europe, and let's not mention the bloody Tories. God help us.' Geoff sat on the arm of the couch. 'This is not who I used to be, you know. Not at all. I used to throw caution to the wind and stay up all night meeting girls, smoking dope. You kind of get the idea you're not allowed to have fun when you're old, outside of watching *Bake Off* ... I can't remember the last time I did something just for the hell of it. Why is acting out only for the young?' Geoff nudged Blakey. 'Besides, we don't have to hurt anybody, do we?'

'And don't worry,' Finley said, 'I've seen it on TV a million times, well, when my TV was working anyway. How hard can it be?'

Blakey despaired. 'Ocean's Eleven we ain't. What am I listening to? And from you, Geoff, of all people.'

'It would be kind of fun to think about it,' Geoff said. 'Like a research project.'

Finley swigged his beer. 'Right then, tomorrow let's scope out the bank on the High Street, the one ol' Derek manages … Aye, that's the idea.'

'There's no way I'm walking into a bank with a gun and stealing money,' Blakey protested.

Geoff beamed. 'You don't need a gun. None of us do. We'll just pretend.' He pointed a finger from inside his coat pocket. 'Besides, I'm sure the bank's got insurance for this sort of thing, and the staff are trained to just hand over the money, so who are we hurting?'

'You don't even need to walk inside,' Finley said. 'We'll need a driver – that can be you.' Finley put his beer down. The colour had come back to his cheeks.

'Ah, I see.' Blakey smiled. 'I get it; there's no way on earth you two plonkers are actually going to rob a bank.' He laughed out of relief. 'But I'll tell you what, I don't mind sticking around to watch you two buggers clown around. It's bound to be a laugh.'

'So you'll be the driver?' Finley said. 'You got access to a discreet vehicle?'

'Discreet?' Geoff chortled. 'If you call a mustard-yellow 1978 Ford Escort Mk2 discreet.'

Finley rubbed his chin. 'Is it fast?'

'By 1978 standards, yeah,' Blakey said.

Finley slapped his hands together. 'Then it'll do.'

'Wait. I'm more than happy to watch you two have some sort of old-age crisis, but on one condition,' Blakey said. He raised a finger. 'Quid pro quo. Favour for a favour. Here's the deal: I'll hang about while you get this idea out of your system, cos at least it'll get you out of the house and help bring you back to life, but in return all three of us have to come back here and clean up this mess of a flat.'

'Deal.' Finley raised his can. 'All hail the High Street Bandits! Tomorrow morning, we'll scope out the bank.'

'Oh, I'm not sure I can do it tomorrow,' Geoff said. 'I've a dentist appointment in the morning.'

'Told you,' Blakey said. 'I knew he'd bottle it.'

Geoff puffed out his cheeks. 'Oh, sod it! Sod the dentist, and sod the hotpot too.' He reached into Finley's box of Carlsberg and pulled out a can.

'All hail the High Street Bandits!'

CHAPTER ELEVEN

Blakey's car purred as he slipped it into third and cruised towards Glebe town centre. Its roof shone like a mirror and its wheel arches glimmered with polished chrome trim. The car was an impressive vintage machine, always sure to turn more than a few heads as it cruised down the street. Good progress was being made on their journey, until the temporary traffic lights on Rockwell Street stopped them.

'There's always roadworks going on around here,' Geoff said from the rear seat.

'Aye, they're always ripping it up and starting again,' Finley said.

A sharp screeching filled the air as the jackhammer pounded the tarmac in front of Finley's window, like a multitude of metal drums all beating in sync. A man in a high-vis vest and ear defenders was barely visible through the dusty cloud of debris kicked up by the hammer.

'It's so different around here now,' Blakey said. 'Remember the old playing field that used to be up here? The one that backed onto Murray's farm. The entrance used to be about there, where Poundland is.'

'That was the one we used to go raspberry picking in, on the way home from school, wasn't it?' Finley said.

'And there used to be a pub just here' – Blakey pointed up the avenue – 'The Unicorn. When I was about eight or nine there was no such thing as high-street bookies, so my nan used to save up all week, then on Saturday she'd give me three pence and send me to the pub to put her bets on. The bookie used to park round the back in this beautiful Jag. I'd add my bets to the bottom of my nan's slip and put my one penny in with her money before I handed it to the bookie. He'd give me one of those little smiles that old men used to have, where the dimples on their cheeks cut through their wrinkles, and sometimes he'd sneak me a bottle of beer for my trouble. I wonder what happened to him.'

'He'll be long gone by now,' Finley said. 'Just like the cobbled streets and the Odeon. I used to go see a film at the old cinema at least once a week. You could spend all day in there, watching the cartoons, then the main feature.'

'Do you remember *The First Man Into Space*?' Blakey said.

'Do I ever.' Finley smiled. 'With that crusty-looking monster that kills everybody. Oh, and I loved *Devil Girl From Mars*. She was my first crush. Cracking picture, that.'

The conversation died down and Finley looked lost in space as he stared out of the window, his view fixed on a homeless person who'd set up camp in the glass shelter of a bus stop. The homeless man was wrapped in layers of ragged clothing, with a sleeping bag draped over him like a cloak. Blakey imagined

Finley huddled in that corner, stranded and destitute with no protection from the elements, and wondered how he'd survive. Judging by Finley's fallen expression, Blakey felt sure he was having the same thought.

The temporary lights turned green and they moved swiftly along.

'Good to know the Monkey's is still open,' Geoff said as they passed it. 'That's the first boozer I went into when I moved to England.'

'Good pub that. I've not been in the Monkey's for donkey's,' Finley said.

'I'll treat you to half a mild,' Blakey said, 'if you reconsider this crazy idea of yours.'

'Here it is. On your left,' Finley said. 'Just pull into the disabled parking spot out front.'

The bank and its high-class exterior came into view. Marble pillars flanked the entrance, and signs in the window encouraged people to come in and enquire about overdrafts and mortgages. Blakey parked beside two cash machines by the roadside.

'What are you hoping to find inside? You know what a bank looks like,' he said.

'We'll just look around and get a feel for it. That's not illegal. No one can arrest us for looking,' Geoff said.

'Depends on what you're looking at, I suppose,' Blakey said, chuckling.

'Bollocks to it,' Finley said. 'Since we're here now, we're not going to just case the place. Absolutely not, we need to be more assertive than that. We need to seize the day. Grasp the nettle. Er, ride the cow.'

'What?' said Geoff.

'Listen, we're the High Street Bandits, so let's just go for it. Let's get in there and rob the bugger!'

'You must be mad.' Blakey turned to the back. 'You really are off your rocker, aren't you? I thought a ride into town would have calmed you down.'

'Carp demin,' Finley said.

'It's carpe diem,' Blakey said. 'And I don't remember you being this stupid.'

Finley turned to Geoff. 'Don't listen to him, mate. All we need to do is walk inside, go to the counter and demand the money. It's that simple. They'll never see it coming from a couple of old fellas like us. Let's not waste time. Come on, let's just get on with it.'

Geoff tried to speak, but Finley stopped him.

'Less talk, more action – that's how things get done. Look, I brought these.' Finley produced two bags-for-life from inside his coat and pushed one into Geoff's hand. 'These are to put the money in.'

'You can't be real,' Blakey said.

'Real as mustard,' Finley said, smiling. 'You got a full tank of gas, yeah?'

'If you mean petrol, I think so. I never did get round to fixing the fuel gauge.' Blakey tapped the dial.

'Righto. Keep the engine running.'

'Aren't you forgetting something?' Blakey said.

Finley looked about.

'Masks – balaclavas, hoods, bandanas,' Blakey said.

'Oh, what a shame,' Geoff said, relaxing back in his seat. 'He's right, you know. We don't have any masks, so it looks like that's that. Never mind.'

Finley thought for a second. 'I have an idea. Let's just put our shirt collars up high and tuck our chins in, then when we're at the counter we'll just hide our faces with our hands.'

Finley popped his collar and held a hand over his chin.

'Foolproof,' Blakey sniggered, but Geoff didn't look convinced. When he tried popping his collar and tucking his neck in, he looked like a turtle in retreat.

'It's now or never,' Finley said. 'Let's go go go!' Finley harried Geoff out of the car and nudged him along the pavement. Blakey watched them shuffle towards the bank with the bags-for-life dangling from their fingers. Finley went straight inside, but Geoff stopped to glance over his shoulder. Finley yanked him inside.

Oh 'eck, what if they actually do it? Blakey thought. Maybe I should have taken the whole 'rob a bank' idea a bit more seriously. It's definitely a cry for help.

He felt suddenly suspect, sitting in his yellow car in the street outside. He looked about. Maud from the post office was at the cash machine. He gave her a little wave and sank into his seat. He checked the fuel gauge again, tapping the dial, and kept his eyes on the street. His mind wandered. How long could he park before he got a fine? There were no parking signs that he could see. How much fuel do you use when you keep the engine idling for so long?

He was just about to nod off when Finley and Geoff dashed out of the bank, bags swinging, faces flushed. They ripped open the passenger doors and dived into the car.

'Bloody hell! I didn't think you'd actually go and do it.' Blakey revved the engine, took off the handbrake, and with a thunk, stalled the engine. 'Bugger! Wait a second. Hold on.'

'Never mind, don't bother,' Finley said with a sigh.

'What happened? You get the money?' Blakey asked.

'Well, I got a bit of stage fright so I got Geoff to approach the counter.'

'And …?'

Geoff's collar was still up and he was holding his breath. With a burst, he finally exhaled. 'I was nervous, but when I got in there, I felt ready to go for it. I felt bold. So I walked by the reception desk, past the sign that says "Ask us about our overdrafts", and walked towards the counter, you know, where all the money is.'

'Then …?' Blakey said.

'Well, what I wanted to say was "Give me all your money", but what I ended up shouting was "Tell me about your overdrafts!".'

Blakey slapped the steering wheel and howled. He couldn't catch his breath. 'Ronnie Biggs, eat your heart out!'

'Yeah.' Geoff puffed out his chest. 'But I got a cracking deal on an overdraft. Two hundred quid.'

Blakey wiped a tear from his cheek. 'Just do that fifteen times and you'll solve all Fin's money problems, no bother.' Blakey caught sight of himself in the mirror; he was beetroot red from laughing. 'Oh, bugger me.' He chuckled.

'Right then,' Finley said, not finding any humour in the situation. 'We'll come back later this week for take two.'

'No chance,' Blakey said. 'Geoff's lost his nerve already.'

'No, I haven't,' Geoff said.

'Both of you have, just admit it,' Blakey continued. 'If you were going to rob the place, you'd go back in and do it now, wouldn't you? But you've bottled it, which is no bad thing. This was a terrible idea to begin with and I'm glad you've come to your senses.'

'Nah,' Finley said. 'It's not about sense, it's about the fact that two bank visits in ten minutes is a bit suspicious. Nobody does that.' He folded his shirt collar down. 'We need to lay low and pick our moment, otherwise we'll give away our intentions. Besides, it's a bigger job than I thought; they had security cameras and everything in there.'

'Yeah, I saw them too,' Geoff said.

Blakey rolled his eyes. 'Of course they have cameras. What did you expect?'

'It's not like in the movies,' Geoff conceded.

'Look, we just need to case the place properly and figure out where all the security cameras are,' Finley said. 'Like I mentioned, if we plan this right no one will suspect that three old geezers turned this place over. So, with that in mind, when we go in and do the job proper we might need to move and act young while we're in there, you know, to throw 'em off our scent.'

'That should be easy for you two,' Blakey said. 'I'm sure Geoff can just forget about his bad hip.'

'Okay, okay,' Geoff said. 'Let's come back another day and have another look inside, just to prepare us for any unexpectedly large signs or good offers. It's distracting, all that stuff, you know.'

Finley smiled. 'Sounds like a plan. Let's aim to be ready so we can turn the place over on Friday.

Friday's just as good a day as any and we'll avoid the weekend foot traffic.'

'In the meantime,' Blakey said, turning to Finley, 'I think we ought to move on to part two of our agreement.'

'What's that?' Finley said. He'd always been bad at playing dumb.

'The only way I'm going to bring you back here is if we all make a start on cleaning up that pigsty of a flat.'

CHAPTER TWELVE

Returning to Finley's flat, Blakey noticed the old bird feeder on the tree stump had fallen down. Finley picked it up and tried to put it back, but all he could do was wedge it into a split in the stump and leave it standing at a wonky angle.

'All I need now is some seed to put in it,' Finley said, staring at the teetering, seedless feeder. His lips flattened to a line and he shook his head. Then he pulled out his keys and walked to the door.

The flat was worse than Blakey remembered, and colder too. Finley wasn't kidding about having the heating cut off; it was just as cold inside as it was out. Ah, still, he was here to do a job, a favour. But, although he had mentally prepared for the task, he'd failed to prepare in any practical way: he should have brought gloves, bin liners, cleaning sprays and other things of that ilk. Bugger. It was going to be a long day.

'First things first,' Finley said, 'I'll get the kettle on. And by that I mean I'll boil some water on the camping stove I've got set up in the kitchen.'

'Okey-dokey,' said Geoff. He scratched his flat cap and blew out his cheeks. 'Hard to know where to start, isn't it?' He pointed at the stricken silver TV lying across the couch. Its bezel was still adorned with an 'HD ready' sticker, yet it was apparently ready for the scrapyard. 'Eh, Finley, that telly: what's wrong with it?'

'Doesn't power on,' Finley said above the sound of clinking cups and flowing water. 'I've only used teabags, and no sugar or milk.'

'I'll take away the telly,' Geoff said as he picked it up and set it by the door.

The pictures on the wall, reproduction watercolours depicting landscapes, were grey with dust. Even the skirting boards were covered in grime. An ironing board was set up but piled high with books and DVDs, all covered in the same layer of dust. Blakey needed to start somewhere, so he grabbed one of the several empty Carlsberg boxes and rifled through the rubbish tip that was the coffee table.

He looked at the date of one of the many newspapers piled up. Thursday, 2 April 2021, over two years old. On the front was a picture of a baroness in a swimsuit with her sunglasses on, posing on the deck of a yacht. 'Bra Queen Claps Nurses While Defrauding the NHS for Millions', the story read. It went on to accuse the Tories of cronyism in relation to handing out massively profitable contracts to those with connections to the government. Blakey shook his head and wanted to ball the paper up, but another story caught his eye. It was about a thirty-year-old man who'd sailed around the world and was struck by how lonely the experience was. Imagine travelling all that way on purpose, Blakey thought, and all that expense, just to come home and say you were lonely. What did he expect? Parties in the galley with the support crew? If he thought one hundred days in a boat was lonely, he should try doing a decade in an old folks' home. Blakey crumpled the newspaper and chucked it into the empty beer box and busied himself with the letters, sorting them into two piles: one for the regular-looking post and one for those marked 'Final Demand' and 'Urgent'.

After this scant effort, and having sized up the job a little more, Blakey realised that he had no idea what to do next. So when Finley came back with the tea, he decided it was time to take a hardly earned break and sat next to Geoff on the now fully accessible two-seater couch.

'Looks better already,' Finley said, easing himself into his armchair. 'Gonna need a hoover, though.' He signalled to the bric-a-brac behind the front door. 'Mine broke a while ago but we can borrow one from number 20 next door. She's alright, is Daisy.' He sipped his tea. 'But you needn't bother with all this, you know.'

'I said I'd help,' Blakey said.

'And I did too,' Geoff said. 'We old boys need to stick together.'

'Aye,' Finley said. 'Aye … Er … Never mind.'

'What?' Blakey said.

Finley stared into his mug. 'Nothing, nothing. It's just … well, you know … thank you. To both of you.'

A wood pigeon fluttered by the window. The bird inspected the empty feeder and flew off.

'I'll get the hoover from next door,' Geoff said. He left Blakey and Finley examining the contents of their mugs.

CHAPTER THIRTEEN

'It's only a bloody Gtech AirRam!' Geoff said as he returned with the vacuum. 'Powerful, these are. It should sort the carpet out in no time. And next door gave me these.' He showed off a plastic box full of cleaning paraphernalia. 'There's carpet cleaner in here, and Dettol, and Flash multipurpose spray, bin bags, rags, and even some new sponges. And I tell you what, that Daisy next door is some lady.'

'Oh aye,' Finley said. 'You've got a spring in your step all of a sudden. I thought you were married.'

'Divorced.'

'Ah, sorry,' Finley said.

'We're better apart than we were together.'

'You married, Blakey?'

Blakey was shuffling the coffee table to one side of the room so Geoff could use his powerful new toy.

'Yeah, fifty years.'

'Kids?'

'Just one. He's a spark by trade.'

'Grandkids?'

'Yeah, one of them too.'

Geoff powered on the vac and started singing and prancing as he mowed the carpet, doing his best impression of Freddie Mercury.

A smile twitched on Blakey's face as he attacked the windows with a healthy squirt of Flash and a clean rag, streaking them up a treat.

Finley busied himself with bin bags, tossing clothes from the mound in the bathroom into them, then dumping the plump bags by the front door as Geoff took the hoover on a tour of the flat, making sure to get the loose cobwebs off the ceiling and the crumbs off the couch and chairs.

When he was done and the whir of the machine had died, the room was quiet with the kind of relief that only comes after a solid thirty minutes of vigorous cleaning.

'When you're smiling ...' Blakey sang as he buffed the pictures on the wall. 'Oh, when you're smiling ...'

'The whole world smiles with you,' Finley crooned.

The cleaning hummed back into gear and most things ended up in bin bags, apart from the cups and cutlery, which were cleaned and put away. The clothes that were worth keeping were set aside to be washed, and the ironing board was folded up and put in the small storage room. It took a while but even the skirting boards gleamed after a wipe with Dettol and a sponge. The final big job was the bathroom, but to Blakey's surprise, after the old laundry was removed it wasn't too bad. After a few hours he felt exhausted but satisfied by his efforts.

The flat was much better, homely even, but there were two small cardboard boxes taking up space under the coffee table. Blakey picked them up and set them on the decluttered table.

'I think we've done a fine job, even if I say so myself,' Blakey said. 'Shall we sort these boxes out and call it a day?'

'No, no … Not those.' Finley's voice trembled.

'Might as well. We're on the home straight.'

Finley's face grew tight around the eyes and he retreated to his armchair. 'No,' he whispered. 'Not those. Not right now.'

Looking closer at the two boxes, Blakey saw the words 'Ella's Things' written on the side in blue pen. He put them back on the floor and slid them under the table.

'In that case,' Blakey said, 'if I remember correctly, I promised you half a pint.'

Finley nodded. 'That you did, pal. That you did.'

The boys made merry in the Monkey's like it was 1967 all over again, until Finley's legs started to wobble and he had to stagger home. But he smiled as he ambled the short distance. Upon entering his flat he flicked on the light and marvelled at the cleanliness of his home as he fell sound asleep, still wrapped in his coat. It was always easier to sleep after a drink, he thought as he drifted off. It really does help keep the cold at bay.

CHAPTER FOURTEEN

Young lads in football gear jogged across freshly cut grass. They stopped in the centre circle and faced their coach. With ball in hand, he remonstrated for reasons that couldn't be heard and blew his whistle, prompting the players to take positions across the field. But it looked like training had come too early for some of Glebe Town's reserve players, judging by the amount of yawning that was going on.

There was a strict 'no visitors' policy at Glebe Town training sessions, but any dog walker, jogger or concerned grandparent could get a perfect view through the wide slats in the metal fence.

'Looks like it's a six-a-side game,' Finley said as he shivered with Blakey on the other side of the training ground's perimeter.

Blakey watched the ball ping-pong around at slow speed then spill into no man's land. The players gave chase, scrambling and tripping over each other before catapulting the ball out of play.

'Be honest,' Blakey said. 'I know you've got all these money worries, but this bank-robbing talk is just a lark, isn't it?'

Finley's breath was heavy in the air. 'Put it this way, it's either a bank job or a lottery win, and I've no money to play the lotto.'

Blakey didn't want to lecture Finley again about how a bank job was clearly illegal and definitely doomed to fail. Sometimes people deal with problems in strange ways, he knew that. One time, when a neighbour complained that Blakey's garden shed was an eyesore, he got so mad that he painted it pink. A pink shed on Woodhouse Lane! Can you believe that? But he proved his point – it was his garden and his shed and he could do what he liked with both. Until he demolished the shed. Blakey hated pink.

So, if Finley wanted to talk more about his fantasy, his magic bullet cure to his money woes, Blakey would listen. All this was a cry for help, and although Blakey couldn't pay off Finley's debt – he'd already talked through the options with his wife and found his means limited – he could be a friend and just be here for him. It was therapy, he supposed, and it was the best he could do.

'Imagine having all that Euromillions rollover money,' Finley said. 'And imagine all the things you could do with it.'

'I'd buy a few old Jags, me.' Blakey imagined himself in an E-Type, cruising up the M6 and hitting the winding roads of the Lake District.

'Nah, not me,' Finley said. 'I'd have stopped and helped that homeless lad we saw on the way to the bank the other day. I'd have seen him okay. Paid for him to have a week in a shelter. Then I'd buy this football club and turn it into something good, a real winning team, and I'd give the homeless folk around here groundskeeper training and handyman work.

And obviously I'd pay off my debts. My bloody debt …' He shook his head. 'I can tell you've never had debt, Blakey. Not like this: life-threatening debt. It haunts you all the time. It won't let up. It's behind your eyes when you wake and demands answers when you try and sleep. I can't take joy from anything with this looming over me. Dear me … You laugh at the idea of me robbing a bank, and I know it wouldn't make me a millionaire, let's be clear about that, but it would give me something, and something's more than nothing.'

A whistle pierced the air and the coach started shouting again. It looked like the ball wasn't being passed around to his satisfaction. And to be fair, he wasn't wrong. Judging by their performance, it looked to Blakey like some of the players must have had their boots on the wrong way around. Play resumed and Charlie looked like he wanted to make his mark with a moment of possession and a shot at goal, but he accidentally booted the ball a mile over the net and into a neighbouring garden.

'That's my Charlie,' Blakey said. 'Number 78.'

'Big unit, isn't he? But his shooting's diabolical and he's got no fundamentals at all. The coach wants sacking if he's been coaching Charlie for … how long now?'

'About four years.'

'And Charlie's supposed to be a winger?'

'Yeah, like you were.'

'He's big, athletic, fairly quick, but he clearly doesn't know where he's supposed to be on the pitch. The coach needs to tell him to get chalk on his boots when his team's attacking; get right on the defender's shoulder – the least he'll do is pull a player out of position, best he'll do is get the ball and make something happen. But what does an old fart like me know?'

'A sight more than this coach by the sounds of it,' Blakey said. 'Come on, Fin, have a word with Charlie and give him some ideas. Rumour is, at the end of the season he's going to be dropped completely and that'll be his career over.'

Finley put his hands in his pockets and sighed.

'I tell you what, quid pro quo,' he said, 'a deal for a deal: I'll train him if you drive me to the bank for another recon mission tomorrow.'

Blakey nodded. 'Deal.' No harm in looking, he conceded.

'Tell your lad to come over to my place after training. And tell him to bring his boots, a football, a big bottle half full of water, a tennis ball and a roll of toilet paper.'

'Okay, but how's it going to work? You don't have a net or much grass at your place.'

'And neither did George Best when he was a nipper. It's all about technique and how you read the game. So don't you worry, I'll whip him into shape.'

Once home, Finley bypassed his armchair and his box of Carlsberg and went straight to his utility room. He dug around in the back and pulled out a storage box from deep within. The box was heavier than he remembered but, then again, everything was heavier these days.

He put it on the coffee table and fell into his armchair to take a breath and admire the cleanliness of the flat again. For so long the mess had weighed on his mind, and the weight had grown too heavy to bear. But now the place was clean and he accepted that he couldn't have done it alone. He pledged to keep everything in order; he wouldn't let his friends down. Money on the other hand, impossibly heavy. A dead weight. How had it got this bad? How had things got so expensive, and when did he fall behind? He tried not to think about what he owed to the electricity, the gas, the council tax, et cetera, but he wondered how long the queue at the foodbank would be this week.

He reached into the storage box on the coffee table and pulled out his old Youth Cup final jersey. It was just how he remembered it. It probably still fitted. He might try it on later. Underneath, he found his old boots and an album of newspaper clippings documenting his glory days, all in black and white. 'Local Teen Biggest Prospect in North' was the headline on the back of the *Glebe Observer*, 2 May 1964. 'Big Clubs Come Knocking for Wonder Winger, Aged 15' was the story on the back page of the *News of the World*. That one was national press and he was proud of it. The piece was accompanied by a picture of him kneeling by a ball, and another one of him in action, scoring the winning goal in the final. He could still remember that goal, the sound of his boot hitting the ball as he pulled the trigger, the way the goalkeeper dived, the way the net shook, and the way the crowd exploded around him. And on the page overleaf, there he was, centred in view, lifting the Northern Youth Cup.

He couldn't decide if the images made him happy or tearful. It seemed unhealthy to dwell on a life long gone. His mind turned to Ella and he glanced down at the boxes under the table, full of the things she left behind.

The door buzzed.

About time. He wiped his eyes, got up and checked the camera feed on the high-tech security panel by the door and pressed the button on the intercom.

'Stand by, caller, I'll be out in a second.'

He grabbed a game of Subbuteo from the bottom of the storage box and went outside.

'You're Charlie and I'm Finley.' He shook Charlie's hand. 'Your grandad tells me you're a footballer.'

'That's right,' Charlie said with a smile.

'Well, you're not going to be one much longer if you keep training like you are. I watched you today.'

Charlie bounced the football he'd brought. 'It's a hard game this, you know.'

'Don't be ridiculous. It's a child's game, so don't make excuses.'

Charlie shook his head. 'Look, I know you used to play at school an' all that, but this is the professional, modern game. Things have changed a lot since your day. I've only come here cos Grandad said that I better come or else. But I'm not really sure why you asked me over.'

'Because you've got more pace and more height than I ever had, but I was twice the player you are.'

Charlie's head dropped. Finley put an arm around him.

'You've got all the assets to be a decent player. You just need a few pointers to put it together at the right time and in the right place. So, if you're up for it, I'll help you. But promise me you'll practice what I show you every single day, and twice a week you'll come over for more training.'

Charlie sighed. 'At this point, I'll try anything.'

'Right. We're going to use Subbuteo to discuss your position on the pitch and how it changes depending on the state of play so you'll understand how to exploit space on the wing to either cut inside and shoot, or hit the byline and deliver a cross. We should work on your dribbling and shooting first, cos goals are what you need to stay in a job. If you score a few, they'll soon offer you a new contract.'

Charlie held out the bottle of water he'd brought. 'And what's this for?'

'Target practice. You need to be able to hit the toes of your striker, or any square of net, from distance. And the tennis ball is to practise your first touch.'

'And the toilet roll?'

'I ran out this morning. Now get your boots on and I'll be back in a bit.' He took the loo roll and walked back inside.

CHAPTER FIFTEEN

With Finley being so insistent on going back to the bank, Blakey thought he'd humour him again. They did have a deal after all. That's why, first thing on a cold Tuesday morning, he, Finley and Geoff walked through the automatic doors of Bradley's bank, trying to look as nonchalant as possible. It wasn't dangerous to look, Finley kept saying, unless you've got lasers for eyes. Blakey had to agree, and at least this way he could keep an eye on things and make sure nothing went sideways.

But there was something funny about Geoff, something different. Blakey couldn't figure out what. New shirt? Ah, that was it: he wasn't wearing his glasses … wait, no … he didn't wear glasses. So what was it? Blakey kept a close eye on him.

'Interesting,' Geoff said, gazing up at a corner of the bank's interior.

'What?' Blakey said.

'Just cameras, that's all. Old cameras.' Geoff smiled as he jotted down a series of notes and drew an outline of the room. Then, having scoped out the reception area and the main room, they shuffled across the burgundy carpet towards a series of small desks attached to the far wall to get a better view of the cash counter. Blakey felt less suspicious here, and he figured they'd blend in with the other customers and avoid any questions from the overhelpful staff.

And it was here Blakey figured out what was wrong with Geoff.

'Eh, Geoff, I tell you what's more interesting than cameras.' Blakey pointed at Geoff's head. 'This is the first time in I don't know how many years that I've seen your head. Where's your flat cap? I'd forgotten you had hair. And look at it, all combed and parted, nice like. Must be a good reason for it.'

Geoff puffed out his chest. 'Well, if you must know, I have a date this evening.'

'A date! Wow.' Blakey was shocked. Not that Geoff was unattractive, he hadn't dated in years.

'Never mind that,' Finley said. 'We've got to get ready by Friday, remember? So make a note of that camera above the cash counter.'

'Who's the date with?' Blakey said. 'It's not Daisy who lives next door to Finley, is it?'

Geoff grinned and leaned against the desk. 'When I took her hoover back, she was ever so lovely. She invited me in for Battenberg.'

'Oh, Battenberg, is it? She loves a bit of Battenberg, that one,' Finley said.

'I told her how nice her cake was and she invited me to the bingo tonight.'

'Are you paying any attention?' Finley snapped. 'We're here on an intelligence gathering operation, so look sharp.'

A well-suited, grey-haired man emerged from a back office. Oh no. Not the bank manager, not now,

Blakey thought. He cursed his luck. This was exactly what he didn't want, the bank manager on the prowl – and not just any bank manager, but Derek Onions.

'Fat chance of us gathering much intelligence around here with him about,' he muttered, gesturing to Derek.

'Derek-bloody-Onions.' Finley seethed.

Derek was all smiles, striding across the carpet like he was about to receive a Bafta.

'All I needed was five grand to open Finley's Commercial Laundry Service and he turned me down flat. Didn't even listen to the pitch. He just sat there looking at his nails, then piped up with, "I'm afraid the idea just isn't workable", blah blah. And then started on about how old I was. The idea was bloody workable. If it was one thing, it was workable. He never forgave me for that thumping I gave him at high school, that's what it is.'

'He's always been a piece of work,' Blakey said. 'Always talking himself up and pretending he's something he's not. One time, in geography, he told me that Elvis was his uncle. Imagine that: Uncle Elvis!'

'I couldn't live a lie like that,' Finley said.

'I could barely live an exaggeration,' Geoff said.

Derek glanced across the room and noticed the familiar faces. With his silver hair glinting, fake tan beaming, big smile and ice-white teeth glowing, he sauntered across the room, bringing with him a strong smell of moisturiser.

'Well, well, well ... If it isn't Finley John, and Blake Campbell, and some other bloke I've never seen before in my life.' Mr Onions smiled. 'The three musketeers! Come to make any large deposits? Or apply for any mortgages?' He didn't leave time to reply. 'Look, I know it's chilly outside this time of year but I'm afraid Bradley's bank is not the place to come just to get warm.'

'My name's Geoff, and we're here for good reason.'

'Sure you are,' Derek said, rolling his eyes. 'Now listen, I'm a bank manager, the best bloody bank manager this side of London – I've won awards and everything. I'm so good they won't even let me retire: they can't find anyone as good as me to run this place, you know. And it's my job to know where the money is.' He looked between the three of them. 'I can sense money a mile away, at a glance I can see who has it and who does not, and you three most certainly do not. I can't have three old-timers taking space away from actual customers with actual cash, so if you're looking for advice on what government benefits you're entitled to, you've come to the wrong place. Age UK is just off the High Street. You can ask for directions at reception on your way out.'

Blakey knew from his school days that Finley was not one to take being patronised lightly, especially from someone like Derek, and especially with their history. He prepared to step between them, but Finley's shoulders sagged and his gaze fell to the floor.

'Come on,' Finley said, staring at his feet. 'Let's just go.'

CHAPTER SIXTEEN

Finley had opted to walk home, even if his slow pace meant it would take all day. He wanted the time to clear his head. Besides, there was something he'd been meaning to do. He gathered the last of his change from his pocket and approached a payphone. There weren't many payphones around, and most of those left had either smashed glass or were covered in graffiti, like the one he entered. He felt nervous as he slipped coins into the slot: it was the last of his money, at least until his next pension payment. He dialled the number printed on a letter he'd brought with him and waited.

'Hello, you're through to Energon …' said the voice on the other end of the line.

'Yes, hello. This is Finley John here. I'm calling to—'

'If your question is about your bill, please press one …'

Suppose it is, Finley thought. He pressed one.

'We're sorry. We're experiencing a high volume of calls right now and all of our advisers are busy with other callers. If you'd like a call back within the next 24 hours, please press one … If you'd like to use our automated service, please press two.'

Finley grew nervous about how long the call might take and wondered how much call time £1.45 bought you these days.

'You're through to the automated service. Please use the keypad to enter your account number …'

Finley punched in the digits.

'One moment while we access your account … Would you like to pay your bill by credit or debit card?'

'No.'

'Are you thinking of leaving Energon?'

'No, I'm not. Can I just talk to a—'

'I'm sorry, I didn't catch that. Are you thinking of leaving—'

'No.'

'Are you having technical difficulties with your energy supply?'

Finley's soul grew weak.

'No. I'd like to discuss difficulties with paying my bill.'

'Would you like to hear the current balance of your bill?'

'No,' he whispered, too defeated to muster any gusto.

'If you'd like more information about your bill, please visit Energon-dot-com-forward-slash-pay-my-bill. Or chat to us using Mixie, our automated chatbot. Just open Energon-dot-com-forward-slash-help in your web browser and click chat. Thank you for calling.'

The line went dead. Finley couldn't believe it. 'Hello! Hello!' he kept saying into the receiver.

Surely that wasn't it, the sum total of help provided, and the closest he could get to talking to a human being. He slammed the receiver down, hoping to get some coins returned. He checked and rechecked the little coin release box beyond the tiny swing door, but nothing came out. He thought about his options and couldn't think of any, so he left the phone box and went back into the cold breeze for the long walk home.

CHAPTER SEVENTEEN

Geoff had steadied his nerves with a fresh squirt of Old Spice, half a pint of mild and a breath mint before he picked up Daisy en route to the bingo hall. They sat down at what Daisy referred to as her usual table.

'Legs eleven … number four,' cried the caller, triggering jeers from players across the room.

'Are you being rubbish on purpose?' cried one irritated player in the front row who was clearly used to a better standard of calling.

'I'm sorry, Geoff, it's usually better than this,' Daisy said. 'It's the caller's first time. He's only a young lad and we have to blood the next generation somehow.'

Geoff didn't mind. He wasn't even listening to the fluffed calls by the lanky young moptopped lad at the stand. He was just happy to be on a date with Daisy. He was also distracted by the size of the purpose-built bingo hall which was a far cry from the cold church he'd last played in, sometime in the early seventies back home in Stuttgart. This place was a glitzy, exciting, blockbuster of a place with big prizes on show: you could win one thousand pounds on any game or even have your energy bills paid for a whole year, if you played your cards right. You could win a massive hamper of food, too. Meanwhile, purple-shirted staff smiled while bringing over cocktails … And the snacks! No wonder Daisy liked it here.

The surrounding players kept their eyes locked on their venue-provided computer tablets, the bingo graphics lighting up their faces.

'This your new fella?' said Rhonda, one of Daisy's friends.

'He's my new friend. Isn't that right, Geoffrey,' Daisy said.

Geoff could only smile.

'Two fat ladies … twenty-two!' This call elicited hisses from some, banging on tables from others. Someone even threw a handful of chips at the caller, who smiled wryly and was possibly making bad calls on purpose after all.

'Geoffrey?'

'Yes.'

'Next time we meet, maybe we could go to a restaurant together. You know, just you and me, some place we can be alone.' Daisy's lips curled to a smile.

Rhonda raised an eyebrow.

Geoff felt a blush come over him. 'Yeah, sounds good. When do you have in mind?'

'Next Friday.'

'Oh, er.' Geoff felt the temperature rise and loosened his collar. 'I'll have to check. You see, I'm meant to be robbing a bank that day.'

Daisy threw her head back and laughed, her silver curls falling down her back. 'Oh, you are funny, Geoffrey. I do like a man of danger.' She leaned towards him, her brown eyes wide with impish humour.

'I think you should rob a bank another day, cos on Friday maybe you're going to have your hands full with some other hot property.'

Geoff couldn't help but notice Daisy's ample bosom and her low-cut top. He went to take off his flat cap, forgetting he wasn't wearing one. Fortunately, the two glasses of prosecco he'd ordered arrived, along with a bowl of nachos. Risky food, nachos, with all that cheese and jalapeño, but he'd been in a risky mood of late and he was enjoying living dangerously.

He handed Daisy a glass of fizz and said, 'Maybe I can rearrange the robbery, you know … just for you.'

Daisy leaned forward and whispered breathlessly in his ear, 'Oh, Geoffrey, if you did, I would be ever so grateful.'

She held out her glass.

'Cheers.'

And with a clink, Geoff forgot all about his nachos.

And the bank robbery.

CHAPTER EIGHTEEN

Blakey was idle on the water's edge, fishing rod in hand, watching for the telltale twitch of fish on line. The grassy banks of the river were just as fresh as they had been in his youth, and the soil just as damp on the seat of his pants. The water still crested and folded along the current, just as it had done then, and the surface was alive with the same motion, disturbed only by the drop of his lure, but only for a moment, until the ripples radiated and faded. The gentle babble of the water mixed with occasional sighs from Finley as he lay on the grass with his hands behind his head.

'Charlie looked better in training today, didn't he?' said Blakey.

'He's coming along. I taught him the ol' shimmy shake, you know, the drop-the-shoulder, leave-the-defender-standing routine.'

'Aye, he did that today. Left his man for dead, he did. Bagged a cracking goal off the back of it too. And the coach seemed impressed; he even stopped shouting for a second.'

'It was my trademark move, that was,' Finley said, his eyes still closed. 'Got me plenty of goals. And he's a quick learner, your lad. Still a long way to go, but if he keeps at it, he'll get somewhere.'

Blakey felt a swell of pride.

'Ah, he'll be a player yet,' he said. 'And I'm glad you came with me today. The idea of fishing on my own has always made me feel so depressed I haven't held a rod in years.' Blakey kept his eyes on the water, hoping to see his fishing line tremble.

Finley had no rod, nor any apparent interest in one. It seemed like he was just enjoying the breeze across his face.

'It's no big favour to come out into the fresh air and relax in the sunshine,' Finley said. 'Especially after the way you helped me with the flat. Now, stop being soppy, you, and get a fish caught.'

The two men took in the daylight. After some time, Finley whispered, 'I'm glad we met again after all these years.'

'Aye, me too.'

'To think so much time has passed since we were lads, although I don't feel much older really, truth be told.'

'I don't think you've changed one bit, deep down,' Blakey said. 'And that's a good thing. Despite the troubles you've got at the moment, you're still the guy I knew.'

Finley sighed. 'You know, sometimes I think the only difference between young and old is the amount of pain you carry with you.'

Blakey got lost in thought but found his way back.

'Do you remember when you dared Barry Hathaway to eat those urinal cakes?'

'Ha ha! What a rotten beast he was.'

'That was at the party we held to celebrate you winning the Youth Cup.'

'It was.'

'You scored a hat trick in that game; you were man of the match too, do you remember?'

Finley chuckled. 'Of course I remember. I've still got the match day jersey at home. And clippings from the paper.'

'Hell of a party that was afterwards.'

'It was drinks all round, and it felt like the whole town was crammed inside that pub. That was the night I met Ella.'

'Ah, I remember. You couldn't keep your eyes off her.'

'That's why I married her. And that pub was where it all began. I proposed to her in that same pub years later, cos I knew what we had would last a lifetime. Thank God I met her.'

'It wasn't long after that party that we lost touch,' Blakey said.

'I suppose so. It's funny how life can take you off in all directions, and how you can get so preoccupied and forget what's important when you have youth on your side.'

The river's surface floated by.

'That's the thing about fishing,' Blakey continued, 'it really gives you time to relax, to think and reminisce. You can come out here and slow it all down for a while. And with any luck, all this peace and quiet will get that robbery madness out of your head.'

Finley opened his eyes. 'Who says I want it out of my head? You're still up for being the driver, right?'

Blakey took a breath so he could measure his words. 'Of course I'm not going to be a bloody driver for a bank robbery!' He didn't mean to raise his voice; he just measured his words wrong. He couldn't be involved in a bank job; it was just not who he was or ever wanted to be.

Finley bolted upright. 'Hey, you – we had a deal.'

'And what happens when we get caught thirty seconds after leaving the bank? What then? Jump on the next flight to Brazil?'

'Don't be daft. People get away with bank robberies all the time, 'cept you don't hear about it in the news cos they don't want to encourage others. They never report the successful robberies, only the ones that are foiled.'

'Cooee,' a voice hollered behind them, and a silver-haired, lime-green lady appeared at the crest of the hill, striding with a hamper over her wrist. Geoff ran alongside, chasing his flat cap across the grass as it rolled in the wind.

'What's Daisy doing here?' Finley said.

'I think they're an item now. I called Geoff this morning to see if he was coming fishing and she answered,' Blakey said.

'Fair dos.'

'Hello boys!' Daisy removed her sunglasses and waved. 'I've brought refreshments.'

Geoff finally got hold of his cap, pushed it on his head and took a seat by Finley.

'Alright, fellas? Fine day for it.'

'Fine day for what?' Finley said.

'Cheer up, you old sod.' Daisy reached inside her hamper and produced a bottle of oatmeal stout and a bottle opener. 'I thought this might cheer you up.' She handed them to Finley.

Finley winked. 'My dear Daisy … I can't believe I ever underestimated you.' He opened the bottle. 'And Geoff, get this: Blakey here says he's not going to be our driver for the you-know-what.' Finley tapped the side of his nose.

'Oh, you needn't speak in code,' Geoff said. 'Daisy knows that we were thinking about robbing a bank.'

'Ah, bloody hell,' Finley said. 'Tell you what, it's a good job you don't work for MI5. What if she were a copper?'

Daisy smiled. 'Oh, I'm no copper, but I do own handcuffs.'

Geoff's grin almost split his face.

'Wait a second, Geoff,' said Finley. 'What do you mean you told her we were thinking about robbing the bank?'

'Well, I've been thinking …'

Finley screwed up his face. 'Oh, not you an' all! We had a deal. We all had a deal, the three of us. I can't do this on my own.'

As much as Blakey felt bad, he didn't feel bad enough to become a criminal. 'We'll think of another way to sort your money situation out, lad.'

Finley put his head in his hands. 'We've been through this. I've already told you I'm all out of ideas and all out of time.'

'We just need to have a good think and come up with a better plan— Oh blimey, what's that!' Blakey's fishing line jumped and his rod lurched forward. He couldn't believe it.

'A bite! I got a bloody bite,' he shouted.

'Well done,' Geoff said.

'What a hero!' Daisy said.

Blakey wrestled with the rod. He couldn't quite remember how to bring in a fish but he knew he shouldn't yank it. He tried to slow himself and gradually reel the catch closer, but it was putting up one hell of a fight.

'Look, Fin,' he said. 'Must be a right monster, this one. Look!' When Blakey turned to him, all he saw was a flat patch of grass where Finley had been lying, and a slumped figure walking off into the distance.

CHAPTER NINETEEN

The fish was a big bugger: it must have been *this* big. The water splashed and sploshed as the beast raised a maelstrom.

'What do we do now?' Geoff cried.

'Get the net,' Blakey yelled.

He pulled the rod back and the pole bent wildly into the river, dragged down by the strength of the fish.

'It's got more bloody fight than me, this thing,' Blakey said, leaning back.

'Be careful!' Daisy handed Geoff the net, but with a crack, the rod snapped and Blakey slipped on the wet grass and tumbled towards the water. He felt Geoff's hand grab the back of his shirt, but it was no good – he fell face first. Cold water filled his sinuses and drenched him from boots to barnet.

Wrenching himself up in the shallow depth, with a bit of effort he found his feet and wiped the water from his face. Despite the cold, a blush of embarrassment burned over him, and the temperature got higher when he saw Daisy and Geoff red with laughter, doubled over and pointing. He looked beyond them, hoping to catch a sight of Finley, but he had disappeared from view.

Geoff came to the river's edge. 'Come on, lad. I'll help you out.'

Blakey packed up his broken rod and waved the laughing couple off as he loaded his tackle into the boot of his car. Hell on the interior all this river water will be, he thought as he lined the driver's seat with the shopping bags he kept in the boot. Still damp all over, he wiped his hands and head with the cloth from his glovebox and started off home.

Poor Fin, he thought as he made the short drive. I can't fall out with him already: I've only just reconnected with him. I'll get cleaned up and pay him a visit. He'll have got back to the flat by now.

The temperature dropped and he felt a shiver as he pulled into the driveway of number 114 Woodhouse Lane, a small dormer bungalow that had been home to Blake and Lizzie since they were married in 1967. They'd broken the bank to get it – £2,300 – and it maxed out their budget, but Blakey thought it was worth it for a new build with a garage that he could turn into a workshop.

His wife was waiting for him at the door, which either meant trouble, or that she'd locked herself out again. He'd been meaning to fix that latch.

'What the bloody hell happened to you?' she said as he slammed the car door and walked across the gravel.

'Let's just say I lost the battle of the bass.'

She shook her head. 'What are you like, you big dafty. Come here.' She leaned in for a kiss. 'You'll need to get out of those wet clothes, but first you better get in the kitchen. They've been waiting for you since lunch.'

'Lunch? Since when do we use the word "lunch" in our house? What time's "lunch"? Is it the same time as dinner?'

Lizzie waved him inside. 'Let's just say they've been waiting for a while.'

'Waiting? Who?'

'No no. Go and see for yourself. I tried calling your mobile but it didn't ring.'

'That's odd.'

'There's nothing odd about it, considering it's probably out of battery and locked in your glovebox, as usual. Oh, Blakey, do charge it up and turn it on, for my sake.'

Blakey nodded but his thoughts had already turned to the kitchen. Maybe someone had overheard all the talk of robbing a bank and had called the police. Or perhaps there had been a death in the family, or a close friend had died.

Blakey wiped his shoes on the doormat, in part to get the last of the river mud off, but also to buy a minute to prepare himself for what was in the kitchen, because the kitchen was where big news happened. He expected sad faces, or the police, but instead, stood by the kettle, were Charlie and Robin, wide-eyed and ready to explode.

'There you are, Grandad. We've been waiting for ages. What the 'eck happened to your clothes?' Charlie said.

Robin held Charlie by the arm. 'Never mind that, Charlie. He's here now, so go on ... tell him.'

'Yeah, tell me already.'

'Calm down. I'm getting there. Give me a sec.'

Lizzie walked in and put a towel over Blakey's head.

'Have you told him yet?' she said.

'No, they bloody well haven't. Who's died?'

'Bloody hell, Grandad. No one's died.'

'Arrested?'

'Give over!' Lizzie said. 'When did you become so pessimistic? Now listen, Charlie and Robin have something to tell you. Go on, Charlie.'

Blakey couldn't help but interject. 'Wait a second ... you haven't?'

Charlie beamed. 'I have.'

'You've made the team!'

Charlie rolled his eyes. 'Of course I haven't made the team. Although coach has said I'm getting better. Your mate Fin knows his stuff, you know.'

'So what's all this about then?'

'To be honest, we wanted to have a big party to make this announcement, but we can't wait that long and it would cost money we don't have. So ...'

Robin jumped in. 'Me and Charlie are getting married!' She held out her hand and showed off its new stand-out feature: a golden band complete with diamond.

Blakey inhaled. And kept inhaling. He forgot how to breathe but eventually figured it out. 'Well, blow me down! Congratulations, lad. I always thought you were punching above your weight, so well done!' He hugged Charlie for dear life, then hugged Robin just as hard.

Lizzie took Robin's hand and admired the ring. 'I can't stop looking at it. Some ring that, love. Oh, you're going to be the most beautiful bride.'

'Look at you two,' Blakey said. 'Love's young dream. I'm thrilled for you both, I really am, and you know what? This calls for something special.'

He left the room and had one of those I've-seen-it-around-here-somewhere moments as he rummaged around the garage. Maybe in the corner unit? Aha … there it was. He returned to the kitchen with a bottle of home-made wine that he produced from the plums from the tree in the back garden. It was the first batch from a vintage year: 1967. And with it, he made a toast to the start of a very long and happy marriage.

CHAPTER TWENTY

Drinks and congratulations continued into the night. But as much as he loved them, Blakey was happy to see the lovely couple stagger into a taxi and make the short trip back home. It had been a wonderful but exhausting evening.

Blakey took many questions to bed with him that night: would Will Max, Charlie's dad, be able to afford the lavish wedding plans? Does Lizzie have a stash of money for occasions like this? She'd always been the money expert in the house. But his last thought before bed was, is Finley an early riser?

It went without saying that his visit to Finley's flat had been postponed until the next morning, and having given it some thought he decided that ten a.m. was a reasonable time to arrive unannounced. But fifty-year-old plum wine packs a hell of a punch so an extra lie-in was needed, and by the time he finally got to Finley's, his watch read eleven.

He approached the giant security door but there was no need to use the intercom – the door was wide open. The door leading directly to Finley's flat was ajar too, and there was a man in high-vis standing next to it, sticking what looked like a poster full of oppressive legal text to the door.

'I am sorry,' he said as Blakey passed. 'Honestly, I hate this part of the job.'

Blakey pushed inside, dreading what he was about to face, and found Finley crumpled in his armchair, head down, eyes vacant. The room was empty, totally empty, save for the dimple marks on the carpet where his coffee table, couch and TV stand used to be. Empty squares and picture hooks marked the walls where his watercolour landscapes used to hang.

'The building manager let them in,' Finley said. 'They reckoned they had legal jurisdiction. The only reason they left this armchair is because it belongs to the apartment complex. It's from the common room; the manager let me borrow it cos it's better for my back.'

Blakey could feel Finley's heartbreak from five paces.

'What would Ella think if she could see me now?' Finley's voice wavered. 'Worst part is, I couldn't stop them from taking her things. They just wouldn't listen ... wouldn't even look at me as I begged them to leave her stuff. They said if I had any complaints I should email head office.'

Blakey kept his eyes on Finley. Looking around the room made his blood boil, made him want to cry.

'Morning, fellas,' Geoff said as he walked in. 'I've been over at Daisy's. We had a bit of a lie-in, you might say ... Bloody hell, what happened here?' he said, having finally noticed the empty flat.

'Oh, no,' cried Daisy, who had followed in behind. 'Not ... repossession?'

'Aye, love. Aye.'

'The bastards!' Geoff said.

'And that's not the end of it,' Finley said. 'They need more money, according to the letter they've left. The value of the items was not sufficient, apparently. Blood from a stone they want. They even took my old football shirt and clippings … What are my memories worth to them?' He put his head in his hands. 'The only thing that can help me now is a beer.'

'I'm buying,' said Geoff.

Blakey was too mad to speak. The indignity, the heartlessness. He tried to calm himself down: anger had got him into trouble in the past. Like with the youth in the park not long ago – although he felt his actions were justified on that occasion. Anger could be useful sometimes. But he had to be careful, because his temper had got him into fights he couldn't possibly win. So he kept himself quiet, despite the fact that he felt like a B52 bomber that had just arrived in enemy territory. Tense, and eager for permission to cause damage.

CHAPTER TWENTY-ONE

'They trashed the kitchen too,' Finley said as the boys drank in the familiar surroundings of the Dog and Duck. They had taken a seat by a radiator and were trying to console Finley with a few pints.

'But at least they left my cutlery and camping stove. I guess there's no money in old pots and pans. The flat looks like I've been burgled, and I suppose I have.'

Finley was trying to act normal, but to Blakey, his old friend's physical presence, even the strength in his voice, was diminished. Small and hunched, Finley hadn't stopped hugging himself. Shock will do that to you, Blakey thought. His own feelings were too violent to mention, especially after three pints.

'The government shouldn't allow this. Not to a pensioner with no other income apart from a poxy state pension.' Geoff hadn't stopped fuming, and a few pints in he seemed to be getting angrier by the swig.

Finley attempted to be stoic, but his efforts were betrayed by the need to wipe the corners of his eyes.

Daisy held his hand. 'I'm ever so sorry, Finley. If you need anything, I'm only next door and you can—'

The pub door opened and a shrill voice disturbed the atmosphere. 'Hello, daytime drinkers.'

'Bloody hell, just what we need now,' Geoff said, taking another large swig.

'Derek-bloody-Onions.' Finley shrank and tried to hide.

'He's always around when you don't want him, and always makes himself the centre of attention,' Blakey said.

'What's that?' Derek cupped his ear in Blakey's direction. 'Did somebody call my name? Well, if it isn't the over-the-hill gang.'

Al appeared at the bar, holding up a few large bags. 'It's all here,' he said to Derek.

'Oh, good,' Derek said. 'Be over in a sec. I just want a chat with the old-timers.' He walked over.

'What's in the bags?' Geoff said. 'More money for the bank?'

'It's bags of money for my bank account, if that's what you mean. You see, seven years ago, I had this fantastic idea for a commercial laundry business. It must have come to me in a dream or something because one day – wham! – there it was, a perfectly formed idea, complete with clients, machinery and even premises. I thought, now this is a business idea not to miss. So I took out a business loan, set up the company and put my grandson in charge.' Derek checked his nails. 'These days, I just pick up the bags of dirty tablecloths and whatnots for him every once in a while cos, bloody hell, he's non-stop with all the clients! So, as much as I'd love to stop and chit-chat,

I must crack on. And oh, boys, do me a favour: get that tablecloth as filthy as possible, cos every stain is money, money, money.'

Derek foxtrotted to the bar, collected the laundry and pirouetted out of the door.

'That lying, thieving scumbag!' Geoff said. 'Did you hear that, Finley? Seven years ago he just happened to have the exact same idea for the exact same laundry business that you had. And at the exact same time that you pitched it to him and asked for funding! This is criminal. And the brass neck of the guy to come over here and rub your nose in it.'

'Leave it,' Finley whispered. He gazed at his empty pint. 'I can't do anything about it now.' He closed his eyes. 'You've got to know when you're beaten, and I'm sorry, lads ... but the ref's blown the final whistle.' He rubbed his forehead. 'Seems like the odds were stacked against me from the start, so what the hell can I do about it now?'

Blakey bolted upright and pounded the table so hard ale sloshed out of their pint pots. 'I tell you what we're going to do about it – what we're all going to do about it! We're going to rob that bloody bank!'

CHAPTER TWENTY-TWO

'Shush!' Geoff said, slurring slightly. 'Do you want the whole pub to hear you?'

Blakey scanned the pub. Reassuringly expressionless faces were dotted around the bar.

Finley was open-mouthed. He looked up at Blakey and said, 'You've changed your bloody tune all of a sudden.'

'A reasonable man is allowed to change his mind, isn't he? So drink up.' Blakey necked his remaining mild and pulled the coat off his chair. 'Geoff's right. The walls have ears, so let's move this conversation out of here.'

'I'm not going back to that flat right now,' Finley said. 'Let my soul rest from that wicked sight.'

'Well, we can't go to my place because my missus will be back from Jazzercise by now,' Blakey said.

'We need a place where we won't be overheard,' Geoff said, 'a secure place where we can be sure we can plan this properly without anyone overhearing. A top-secret place that's off the radar and out of the law's reach …'

Daisy grabbed his bicep. 'Oh, Geoff, you big bank robber, you.'

'There's only one place that fits the bill.' Blakey threw on his coat. 'The allotment.'

CHAPTER TWENTY-THREE

'I knew you'd come round in the end,' Finley said as he and Blakey squeezed onto the broken sofa in Geoff's shed. 'You always used to object to having fun till you realised you'd be missing out.'

'My lad did a fine job of patching that roof up,' Blakey said, gazing up at where he'd crashed through the ceiling. It looked like a whole new roof.

While Daisy got comfortable on a desk chair, Geoff finished setting up a flip chart and pulled out a telescopic pointer. 'It's a good job I made notes on our recon mission. Now, enough chit-chat. We've got a job to do, and to do it right we must be prepared.'

'He's suddenly grown a pair,' Finley said through the side of his mouth to Blakey.

'It's funny – he doesn't usually have any kind of accent, but he definitely sounds more German when he's giving orders,' Blakey said.

The two boys chuckled.

'Is there something you'd like to share with the rest of us?' Geoff waved his pointer between the two of them.

'No, sir. It's just that your fly's undone.' Finley sniggered, and that set Blakey off again.

Geoff stood firm. 'And that's just the kind of distracting comment that's going to cost us dearly in the field.' He flipped his chart and revealed the bank's floor plan, drawn in marker pen. 'Observe: cameras are here, here and here, and note the blind spot at the entrance. And just about here, by the counter, we'll be approaching this camera's field of view, so as soon as we get near the desk we'll be on candid camera. But here's the good news: we needn't worry about the CCTV because I happened to note the model of the cameras, and Daisy's grandson was able to find the system's data sheet online and, as I suspected, this rig is an old one. Almost as old as you two. It's ancient tech, based on UHF transmission.'

'Meaning what, Inspector Gadget?' Blakey said, mid-burp.

'Meaning radio frequencies. It broadcasts video over radio signals. And you know what that means?'

'It means I need to go to the bathroom, sir,' Finley said.

'Settle down. You'd think I'm the only one serious about this. It's you I'm trying to help.'

Finley pulled his old coat around him and the smile fell from his face. 'Sorry, Geoff. No more silly buggers.'

'UHF cameras do not like high-powered, wide-spectrum broadcasts at close proximity. It overwhelms the signal and effectively scrambles it. Now guess what my ham radio rig is capable of. Go on, guess.'

Shrugs all around.

'Exactly,' Geoff continued. 'All we need to do is strap an antenna to the roof of Blakey's car and set up an RF amp on the passenger seat. My amp is super-efficient and it shouldn't take much voltage to knock out the camera signal, so we can run the whole system off your car's cigarette lighter. We just need to get you parked up close to the bank – out by the cash machines will do – then we turn on the amp. Then the antenna will broadcast the radio frequencies and it's Scramble City, thank you very much.'

'Cameras shmameras,' Blakey said. 'As soon as we walk inside, people are gonna know it's us, aren't they?'

'Ah!' Finley raised a hand. 'That's where I can help. Been carrying these around in case I found myself in town with enough courage.' He reached inside his coat. 'Hold on.' His hand seemed to get lost within the depths of his pocket. 'Wait, they're in the other one …' He dug his hand into the other side. 'Bloody lining is all ripped … they're stuck … no they're not … here they are.' He pulled out something fleshy, something floppy, unfurled it and stuck in on his head. 'See? Genius. No one will know who we are.'

Blakey stared into Finley's new, distorted yet strangely familiar rubbery face. 'Is that supposed to be a King Charles mask?'

'Think so. They were cheap down the market. They go right over the top of your head and down your neck – complete coverage, so all anyone watching will think is it's King Charles and his twin

brother robbing the bank. No one will believe it. I
didn't want the debt collectors to get these beauties so
I kept them on me so I'd be ready when the time
came.'

'When the time came for what? A coronation?'
Blakey said. 'I'm not wearing one of those. It looks
like you're wearing a condom on your head.'

'You're the driver,' Geoff said. 'Just keep your
head down and you won't need a mask.'

Geoff took a mask and squeezed it on. It wasn't a
perfect fit. His head was a little too big, so King
Charles was smiling manically with his face stretched
across Geoff's. The mask bulged at the top too, like
air was trapped inside.

Blakey shook his head. 'And how exactly are you
going to get them to hand over the money? Just walk
in and say, "Hi, I'm the king and I'd like to make a
withdrawal"?'

'No. I'll just show them this.' Finley struggled
with his pocket again. 'Bloody lining … Like I said,
I'll show them … this bugger!'

'Oh, my bloody stars!' Blakey leapt back and
Geoff started dancing with panic as Daisy let out a
wail.

'Don't point that thing at me!' Blakey yelled.

'Is that what I think it is?' Geoff screamed.

'It's a bloody gun, isn't it? My dad's old service
revolver. I rediscovered it when we cleaned up the
flat. It's decommissioned – he told me he didn't want

a working gun in the house when I was a toddler, so he had the barrel soldered up. He was worried I'd shoot myself by accident, like. Now I keep it in my coat because the streets are dangerous, you know.'

'By 'eck.' Blakey rubbed his temples. 'You really think the money's insured, like you said the other day? And we're not really hurting anyone?'

'We're not robbing a veterans' pension fund,' Finley said. 'Or stealing taxpayers' money, or defrauding the NHS. We're just getting even with that knobhead Derek Onions and getting the debt off my back.'

'So that's the plan,' Geoff said, calming down now, mopping his brow with a handkerchief. 'Antenna on the car. Park close by. Amp on. Me and Finley, I mean Charles and I, go inside. Gimme all your money. Money in the bags-for-life. Leg it. Drive off safely.'

'So brave!' Daisy beamed, and broke into an applause. 'But what if it all goes wrong, my massive, sweet Geoff-cake?'

Geoff pulled off his rubber mask. His face was red, his eyes sullen. The enthusiasm drained from his voice as he took Daisy by the hand. 'My darling, will you come and visit me if I go to prison? My dear petal, will you … will you wait for me?'

Daisy scrunched her face. 'I'm seventy-one. It's a bit late for me to be waiting for owt, so tell you what – just don't bugger it up.'

CHAPTER TWENTY-FOUR

Oh boy. Afternoon had passed into evening and, to nobody's surprise, morning had come, yet it felt like high noon to Blakey. After the meeting, the High Street Bandits took refuge at Geoff's house, and a boozy night in occurred. Beer, whisky, and the sound of Anthony Newley on Geoff's impressive hi-fi resulted in complaints from neighbours. The complaints were turned into invitations to join the party, which led to a whisky shortage. This emergency was eventually resolved by Marie from next door, who nipped back home to grab a bottle of ouzo. Geoff and Daisy smooched, Finley told jokes, cigars were smoked, and a VHS of the 1990 World Cup semi-final was watched.

Now Blakey nursed his hangover by chugging water at Geoff's kitchen sink. The couch was rough to sleep on, and his old bones creaked at the joints, like they always did on bad days. But he had to pull himself together because it had been decided. Today was the day.

Geoff ran into the kitchen, shouting, panicking.

'Calm down,' Blakey said, splashing his face with water from the tap.

'You don't understand,' Geoff said, pacing the floor. 'It's Finley. He's gone. He's not in the spare room and I've searched all over the house.'

'He's probably out in the garden getting some air.' Blakey looked through the window and, through the harsh daylight creeping in through the kitchen blinds, he could see the back garden's immaculate Astroturf. It was empty.

'You know what I think?' Geoff said. 'All that talk of prison yesterday has given him pause for thought and he's bolted.'

'Nah,' Blakey said, wiping his face with a tea towel. 'Even as a kid, if Fin said he was going to do something, for good or ill, he'd do it.'

'You think he's gone to do it alone?'

'No. But I know where he'll be.'

CHAPTER TWENTY-FIVE

Blakey pulled his car into a quiet parking spot sheltered by trees. He turned to Geoff. 'I think I'd better do this alone. This'll be more of an old friend kind of thing, rather than a new friend kind of thing, you know?'

Geoff nodded. 'I just hope he's not done something stupid.'

Blakey left Geoff listening to a Freddie King cassette while he approached the creaky gate that led into the churchyard. He tried to enter as soundlessly as possible, out of respect for the dead and for his old friend, who was kneeling at his wife's grave, sweeping fallen leaves away with his hand.

'I knew I'd find you here,' Blakey said.

'Well done, Columbo.' Finley pushed himself to his feet. 'I've told her all about what we're going to do. Of course, she's not best pleased, but I reckon she'll understand … eventually.'

A handful of fresh posies sat on Ella's grave.

'You know what I'm going to do with my money?' Finley said. 'I'm going to buy a new bird feeder. And feed to put in it, too. Feeding those birds is one of life's few remaining joys, and it makes me feel good to know I'm helping them. We get all sorts around the flat: robins, goldfinches, magpies of course. I saw a bird of prey once. After that, when the birds are fed, I'm going to pay for my funeral. Nothing fancy, like.

All I want is to be put next to Ella. It won't be cheap, but I don't need a party or an expensive coffin. I just need to be by her side.'

Finley took off his watch and held it out. 'And I want to give you this. You know … in case things go wrong. It's the last thing of value I've got left. I couldn't bear to sell it at Cash Generator, which is where most of my valuable stuff ended up when money got short. It was my dad's. He wore it in the war. Now I want you to have it. You never know – it might buy a coffin, should I need one.'

Blakey held the watch. 'I'll be waiting outside the bank for you, not just as a driver … but as a friend. You know that, don't you?'

Finley rested a hand on Ella's headstone. 'Aye, lad. Aye.' He wiped the corner of his eye and sighed. 'Now, enough of the soft lad act. Let's go rob a bank.'

CHAPTER TWENTY-SIX

'Nothing gaffer tape can't fix,' Geoff said, in reference to exactly how he would mount the antenna to Blakey's car. It was a smaller version of the one he had set up outside his shed, but it was still tall, too tall for Blakey's liking, and it definitely ruined his street cred. It was also very likely to attract the attention of the police, but that was a necessary risk, according to Geoff.

With the RF amp set up and the signal generator plumbed in, the three High Street Bandits cruised towards town, masks in hand, bags at the ready, gun tucked in Finley's pocket. Blakey took the long route, to avoid the low bridge at Mettle Alley, through fear of ripping the antenna off.

'You sure that revolver of yours is deactivated?' Blakey said, driving as slowly as he could. 'You're not accidentally going to shoot old Doris behind the counter?'

The whole idea had stopped feeling real to him last night, but now it felt as real as driving a car with a massive antenna strapped to it.

'Don't be daft,' Finley said. 'The cylinder's been soldered up, remember? You can't even get bullets in it, so there's no chance of shooting owt.'

'And this aerial mast, Geoff. What do I say if the police stop me and ask why I have this strapped to my car?'

'Just tell them Radio 4's a bugger to get on an old Escort.'

Blakey shook his head. 'They'll not believe that. Everyone knows you can pick up *The Archers* on a decent set of fillings … I'll tell him it's a fishing rod. It does kind of look like one.'

Down Idle Street, off the corner of Woddledale … the bank was seconds away. The sight of it made Blakey want to hit the accelerator, do a U-turn at the roundabout and head home, laughing the whole thing off as a joke. But he looked at Finley and Geoff in the back and decided to pull in at the cash machines as planned.

'Righto,' Geoff said. 'Now, just flip the switch on the amp, then sit back and wait.'

'And keep the engine running,' Finley said as he left the car.

The street was quiet. No one at the cash machines this time, nor anyone at the bus stop. It was eerie.

'Any enigmatic final words?' Blakey said.

Finley stuck his head inside the driver's window. 'Don't ever go fishing with a radio antenna: it's bound to cause trouble.'

'That's a no, then,' Blakey said.

Geoff and Finley nodded to each other and approached the bank.

This was it: zero hour.

CHAPTER TWENTY-SEVEN

'Right, masks on,' Geoff said, stopping in the doorway.

Finley retrieved his mask from his coat and squeezed it on his head.

'You sure these are made for adults?' Geoff said as he struggled to get inside his.

'You think the camera signal will be scrambled by now?' Finley said.

'I should think so.' King Charles's lips were smeared across Geoff's face, muffling his voice. 'Right now, the antenna is broadcasting high-bandwidth impulsive noise on all channels, just to make sure we've knocked out everything. And as a little bonus, I've sneaked in an episode of *Felix the Cat* on one channel so they have something entertaining to watch when they play back the footage.'

'Right,' Finley said, chafing under the thick rubber. 'Remember, we're not here for mortgages or overdrafts or anything daft. Got it?'

Geoff nodded. 'No overdrafts.'

'Right. Let's practise what you're going to say. Pretend I'm Doris at the till.'

Geoff cleared his throat. 'Okay … here goes … Hi, Doris. Fine day for it. I'm here to rob the bank, so if you could just pop some money into this bag—'

Finley threw up his arms. 'No, you daft apeth! You need to be more menacing than that. Come on!'

'Righto.' Geoff puffed out his chest and dropped his voice an octave. 'Hi, Doris. Give me all your money, please.'

'Close enough, but don't do that with your voice.' He gestured to the door. 'Now come on, let's do this.'

The electric doors opened, and King Charles and his twin approached the cash desk. The bank was empty, aside from Doris who was sitting behind the counter, wearing a mauve shirt adorned with a 'Can I Help You?' pin badge.

Finley steadied his nerves and pushed Geoff towards her. Geoff stood in front of the counter, scratching his neck, trying to catch her eye.

'Ahem,' he said. When that got no response, he tried again. 'Good morning, Doris ... er, I've come to rob the bank.'

Doris was too busy leafing through the newspaper to look up. 'Oh, don't be daft, Geoff,' she said, turning over another page of King Charles's coronation coverage.

'I swear I am, you know,' Geoff protested. 'I'm here to rob the place.'

Doris looked up, paying more attention to him now. She looked him up and down and started to chuckle.

'Bloody 'ell,' Finley cried. 'Why's she laughing?'

'Oh, Geoff, you are funny,' she said. She turned to the back. 'Helen, come and have a look. Geoff's dressed up as King Charles for the coronation.' She beamed at Geoff. 'I'm so glad someone's getting in the mood. It's been all over the papers for weeks, hasn't it? And isn't it exciting! I told Derek to put up some bunting in the bank to celebrate but he said it cost too much.' She rolled her eyes. 'I told him we had some left over from the jubilee, and it's history, this. It's not every day you see a monarch crowned. So, I told him that we should really enjoy it. Well, you know what Derek's like, he just looked at his nails and stopped listening—'

'Wait a second, how do you know it's me?' Geoff said.

'I'd recognise that flat cap anywhere. It's a very distinctive grey.'

Finley facepalmed. 'You had to put your bloody flat cap on, didn't you?'

'We are here to rob the place, I promise you,' Geoff insisted. 'Finley's got a gun and everything. Show her, Finley.'

'Don't tell her my name!' Finley's face was sweating under the rubber. 'Oh, bollocks to it. I might as well now. One sec … it's stuck in the lining.'

As Finley fussed with his ripped pocket, a customer appeared behind Geoff.

'Do you mind if I serve this gentleman behind you?' Doris said.

Geoff moved aside. A scruffy-looking thirty-something brushed past him and slid something across the counter.

'What's this?' Doris said, picking up a folded scrap of paper. She opened it and read it aloud. 'This is a robbery. Give me all your money. No funny business.' She froze.

'Bugger me. We should have done that,' Finley said. 'The old handing-a-note-across-the-counter routine. Keeps it discreet, doesn't it?'

Geoff turned to Finley. 'I think this might be serious.'

The scruffy man banged his fist on the counter. 'Money! Now!'

Doris was rooted to the spot.

With his wild beard and wilder hair, the scruffy man looked like he had a lion's mane. He was tall, lanky, and clearly agitated. He looked over his shoulder and banged on the desk again.

'Come on! Move!'

Doris was wide-eyed.

'Fine,' he shouted and, in one smooth motion, he opened his long coat and pulled a machete out from inside his tracksuit bottoms. 'Have it your way.'

He grabbed Geoff by the neck.

'I didn't want to do this' – he pushed the enormous blade against Geoff's throat – 'but I will. If you don't hand over the cash right now, the old boy gets it!'

'Bloody hell!' Geoff cried.

Doris came to her senses and reached under the desk. In an instant, a barrier fell across the front door and a steel curtain dropped over the serving counter, cutting the three men off from the money and trapping them together.

CHAPTER TWENTY-EIGHT

Blakey shuffled in the driver's seat. 'Come on …
What's taking so long?' He stared at the bank. He
didn't hear any alarms going off, but that didn't
reassure him. Who knew what kind of alarms banks
had? It probably wouldn't be like in the movies, when
a tiny metal hammer strikes an old-fashioned bell
while hooded figures sprint from the bank clutching
bulging bags of cash.

His heart almost stopped when he heard police
sirens in the distance. The high-pitched drone cut the
air, seemingly from all directions, as the ferocious
wail of the law quickly zoomed closer, bouncing off
the walls. A police car came to a halt beside him and
another one stopped in front. Policemen in padded
vests jumped out but didn't pay much attention to him
as he sat sweating in his car's squeaky seat leather.
But he knew they would come his way sooner rather
than later.

A total of six uniforms huddled by a police car
parked across from the bank, and more cars raced
onto the scene with blue lights flashing. The last
vehicle to arrive was unmarked. A woman with a
camera jumped out. It was Rachael Ribbons, the local
reporter who had interviewed Blakey about his
TikTok misfortune.

Blakey rested his head on the steering wheel.
Bugger me, he thought, I've gone from local celeb to

local villain in less than two weeks. I should have known the press would jump on this, but I didn't think they'd be this quick. 'It was a stupid idea anyway,' he muttered. Although, he knew that wouldn't provide much of a legal defence in court. Could Finley's debt be used to persuade a jury? The plight of three poor old men leveraged for sympathy? Probably not.

I'll give myself up, he decided. No sense in running or putting up a struggle – or whatever he could muster that might look like avoiding arrest to a jury. He'd accept that he's been caught, but what the hell would he tell Lizzie? He took his last breath as a free man, stepped out of the car, and waited for his arrest.

CHAPTER TWENTY-NINE

Charlie wasn't on form in training and it was killing him. He just couldn't do anything meaningful with the ball and the more he tried, the more he failed. He had listened to everything Finley had told him, and he had trained for hours every day. There were even a few good showings in front of the coach, so he really thought he'd perfected it: the drop-the-shoulder, shimmy around his opponent, the knock-away sprint-chase, head down, and drive it into the corner. But he just couldn't find the back of the net. He was all too aware that this was the final week of his contract; it was looming over him, and the pressure was too much.

The coach blew his whistle. 'Alright, lads, time's up. Go get your boots clean. I'll see you next week – well, some of you anyway.' He waved Charlie over.

Charlie felt as if he'd been summoned by a ref for a red he didn't deserve. Here we go, he thought, destiny. I'm doomed to be one of those blokes in the pub that gets sloppy drunk and tells everyone the same story about how he could have been a professional footballer.

How was he going to break the news to Robin? Would she still want to marry him? He hoped so, but could they afford it now?

'Son, I know you've worked hard,' the coach said, not looking at him. 'And normally I'd say I could see a future for you in the reserves, but … well, we best have a chat in the office.'

CHAPTER THIRTY

'Calm down, son,' Geoff said as the machete glinted around his neck.

'I don't have to listen to you,' the scruffy man sneered.

'Perhaps not,' Finley said, taking off his mask and stepping in front of him. 'But you're damn well going to have to listen to me.' He clicked the hammer back on the revolver, having finally freed it from the webbing of his pocket.

The scruffy man eyed the pistol. Finley hoped he wasn't a weapons expert. Anyone who knew anything about revolvers could spot a deactivated service pistol from ten yards.

'It's a gun,' Finley said. 'And it's loaded … and it works … so why don't you and me have a little chat, cos no sane person brings a machete into a bank, do they?'

'And what kind of person brings a gun into a bank?' The scruffy man bobbed and weaved on the spot with his arm around Geoff's neck and the blade at jugular height. 'Why exactly do you have that gun, grandpa?'

'My reasons are my own but I suspect they're much the same as yours,' Finley said. 'And I've got news for you, son: I know you. I know who you are. You're Daisy's boy, aren't you? Her grandson, Butler.'

'Daisy's grandson!' Geoff eeked.

Butler tightened his grip around Geoff's neck.

'Calm down, son,' Finley said. 'I know you've not had it easy. Your nan told me all about the hard times. She told me how your dad died when you were young and how your mum struggled with money. Your dear old nan, she helped as much as she could but it wasn't always enough, was it?' Finley looked for a reaction in Butler's eyes and saw nothing. 'Life was hard growing up. And wearing all those worn-out old clothes to school every day only made it worse cos it made you a target for the bullies. I know all about it, son. And it's safe to say that you've had your fair share of troubles.'

Butler stopped looking at Finley. 'Shut up.' He glanced at the steel curtain over the cash counter. 'Where's my money?' he shouted.

'She's a good lass, your nan,' Finley continued, trying to force eye contact. 'So think about how poor old Daisy's going to feel when she hears all about this. Think about how, when your mum was at work and there was no one else around, Daisy took you in. She was always there for you. So, if I were you right now, I'd be a lot more worried about her than any amount of money. Besides ...' Finley glanced at the room and shrugged. 'Look around. There's no money to be had now. It's all locked away behind that barrier – that caught us both out, didn't it? The exit's locked, too, and the police will be here any second ...

so let's face it, the jig's up. The jig's up for all of us …
so why don't you just let my mate go?'

Butler shook his head. 'When the coppers arrive,
they'll have to negotiate with me cos I got hostages.'

'Ah, but you're forgetting one thing,' Finley said.
'I've got the advantage, haven't I?' Finley tightened
his grip on the gun. 'You may have that great big
knife, but I've got a gun. So here's what's going to
happen: I'm going to reach over and put my hand on
that blade of yours, and you're going to let it go.
Understand? That way, when the police arrive, we
can all say that you, in all honesty, gave yourself up.
Which means you're not guilty of anything as serious
as robbery or hostage-taking, and this will all be taken
for what it is: a cry for help.'

Finley took a step forward.

Butler flinched.

Geoff cried out, 'Careful. This guy's not mucking
about!'

'Don't get twitchy now, Butler,' Finley said.
'When people get twitchy, mistakes happen … and
we don't want any mistakes now, do we?' Finley
eased forward a little more. 'You've not being feeling
very well recently, have you? In here, I mean.' Finley
tapped his temple. 'And you've not been able to get a
doctor's appointment cos of the Covid backlog. Your
nan told me that the doctors have kept you waiting for
months cos you're not considered critical.'

Finley stared into Butler's eyes, finally getting eye contact.

'Look at me, son. I know sometimes what's critical can't be seen. And sometimes you can't even talk about it because it's buried so deep down.'

Butler backed up against the counter.

'But we both know that what goes on inside can be just as dangerous as anything on the outside. And just because you can't see it on a scan doesn't mean it's not critical, so you can't keep it all bottled up – my friend Blakey told me that. He taught me that it's okay to ask for help … and you know what, I think he's right. In fact, I know he's right.'

Finley placed a hand on the machete's handle and gently lifted it out of Butler's hands.

Tears streaked down the young man's face as he fell to his knees, sobbing.

CHAPTER THIRTY-ONE

Blakey stared at the pavement, observing every ridge, imperfection, and lump of chewing gum. He didn't dare look up. The waiting was killing him. Just put the handcuffs on me, he thought.

A voice came from over his shoulder. 'Hey up, lad. What you looking at?'

It was Geoff and Finley!

'Bollocksed that right up, we did,' Finley said.

'Aye. Never mind,' Geoff said. 'Let's just go get a pint.'

Blakey felt speechless, but wasn't. 'What happened?'

'Some soppy bugger came in with a machete,' Finley said. 'He stole our thunder but we managed to make him cry, so it all worked out about even.' Finley glanced over his shoulder. 'We better get out of here before the cops collar us for a statement.'

Two police officers emerged from the bank, escorting a man in handcuffs to a squad car as several police vehicles left the scene.

Old Doris stepped outside, clearly in shock. Rachael Ribbons put an arm around her and nodded vigorously while they talked. Then she snapped a pic, and Doris pointed to Finley. Rachael came running over.

'Finley! Finley! You are Finley, right?'

'Depends who's asking.'

'Doris told me that you saved the day in there, had an intervention with the would-be robber. She said you're a hero. I'd love to talk to you. Do you have anything to say to the readers of the *Glebe Observer*?'

'Aye, love.' Finley leaned on Blakey's car. 'Here's an exclusive for you. See, me and my pals here are the High Street Heroes, isn't that right, lads? You can use that in your headline if you like.'

'Smile.' Rachael lifted her camera but Blakey was too confused to pose. And then his phone started to ring.

CHAPTER THIRTY-TWO

'What's that horrible noise?' Finley said.

'My phone,' Blakey said, fumbling with his Nokia. 'Oh, this can't be good. It's Charlie-Boy and he only calls when it's bad news.'

'Answer it, then,' Geoff said.

'Hello. That you, lad? You what? If you're messing with me, I'm going to give you a thick ear cos now is not the time … Nooo! Right, I'm on my way. Make sure you tell your dad!'

'Explain,' said Finley.

'Sounds like another breaking news story,' Rachael said, readying her microphone.

'Geoff. Fin. In the car, now. That was Charlie – they've only gone and called him up from the reserves and put him in the first team for the final!'

'When's the final?' Geoff asked.

'Kick-off in twenty minutes at the stadium.'

'Oh, well, it's no surprise they've called up the reserves,' Rachael said. 'Most of the first team have been struck down by food poisoning. Rumour is they've tracked it down to a bad batch of steak pudding at the chippy on Tibbs Street. And your grandson's in the final now? Wow. Would be a good local interest piece, that. I'm no sports journo but viewing the game through a grandfather's eyes would be a perfect piece for the Sunday edition. Mind if I join?'

'Jump in, lass,' Finley said. 'Geoff, shift the electronics off the passenger seat and throw them in the boot. We've got a game to watch.'

'Charlie better not bugger this up,' Blakey said as he threw open the driver's door.

'Have some faith in him,' Finley boomed. 'He knows what he's doing. And he's a good bloke, too. Just like his grandad.'

The car had never felt quicker but the journey had never felt longer. Skirting the traffic laws, amber-gambling and undertaking, the four of them rode every corner, jumped every bump and only narrowly missed a rogue chicken that was running amok by the stables. At some point, Geoff hit play on the car stereo and Freddie King's 'Going Down' blasted through the speakers. Listening to the hammering piano, the stinging guitar and the husky vocals, Blakey couldn't resist pushing the accelerator to the floor. And when the song finished, the roar of the stadium crowd took over as the floodlights and concrete stands of Musgrave Stadium came into view.

Blakey tuned the radio to catch the match day coverage.

'The scene is set here at Musgrave Stadium for a battle between two of non-league's biggest names, as current champions Garstang FC look to end their impressive season with another trophy win.

Their fans have turned out in force today, with green and white covering the stadium to my right and in front of me. And over in the blue corner, a name from history: a once-great team that has frankly underachieved for the past sixty years. Just to put it into context, their last trophy win was in 1964, in the Youth Cup, and those old enough to remember will have fond memories of an incredible individual performance by young winger Finley John. Boy oh boy, how they could use a little of that magic today. Yes, I'm talking about Glebe Town, whose plucky spirit has caught the imagination of the pundits but whose squad has been rocked by illness, ruling out all but seven first-team players. It's a makeshift side of seniors and reserves, and all conspiracy theories about deliberate food poisoning aside, they have a real challenge on their hands. But shocks do happen, and that's why we love the Lancashire FA Challenge Cup. So stay tuned. Kick-off is moments away.'

CHAPTER THIRTY-THREE

Through the turnstiles and past the pie sellers, Blakey and co were quickly at their seats and shoulder to shoulder with the Glebe Town fans in the upper stand. The game was already under way, as was the jeering and cheering from the crowd. Rachael snapped the scene as Finley took in the view.

'This place hasn't changed a bit in all these years.' Finley was paying more attention to the stadium's girders than the game.

'Is he on the pitch?' Geoff asked.

'He's on the subs bench.' Blakey felt a wave of nerves as he spied Charlie with his boots and match day warm-up jacket on. Charlie looked up and scanned the stands from his seat. He spotted Blakey and waved with a 'Can you believe this?' expression on his face.

'What's the score?' Geoff said.

'Nil–nil. It's only just started,' Finley said. 'Oh, what's this now …?'

The crowd rose to their feet. A player in green and white crossed from deep, launching a looping ball towards a striker. The brute of a player rose above his defender and nodded the ball goalwards. The ball bounced off the post, then bounced off the back of the keeper and bumbled into the net.

'Bollocks!' Finley said. And the other Glebe Town fans agreed.

'How on earth do you know what's going on?' Geoff said. 'Where's the commentary? I've never been to a live match before.'

'Give over,' Finley said. 'It's one-bloody-nil after four minutes, and it looks like Glebe are gonna get a good hiding.'

The Glebe Town manager punched the grass.

Geoff grimaced. 'If I have to watch a bunch of blokes chase a bag of wind, I need some commentary.' He searched his pockets and pulled a device out of his blazer.

'What's that?' Blakey said.

'I never leave the house without a radio. You want to share the headphones?'

'Shush!' Finley said. 'I'm trying to pay attention here.'

Blakey squashed one of Geoff's headphones into his ear and they stood head-to-head, a small length of wire connecting them.

'And Edie breaks loose again down this left-hand side for Garstang, he crosses into the middle, Kundy chests it down. Oh, what a strike! He hit it on the half volley from thirty yards and nearly shattered the crossbar. The ball's gone over for a goal kick but that was some let-off for Glebe Town, who are reeling here, having made a really bad start.'

Glebe fans groaned throughout the first half. But Blakey felt buoyed. After years of watching Glebe Town slide down the divisions, to be only one–nil down at half-time seemed like a result. Pride was all he felt, and even though Charlie was warming the bench, it didn't matter one bit because there he was, a first-team squad player on the day of the final. Finley, on the other hand, was raging; between flashes of frustration, he looked heartbroken and defeated, as if the possibility of Glebe winning the cup was the one last good thing left in his life. The commentator said it best:

'As the referee blows the half-time whistle, there'll be one team that will be glad to get off the pitch and get out of the firing line. It's been a fraught forty-five minutes for Glebe Town, backs-to-the-wall stuff throughout. It remains one–nil here at the Musgrave Stadium, but don't let the scoreline fool you. This game is all but over and Garstang have been imperious. Yes, anything can happen on cup day but if the second half is anything like the first, Glebe's defence will surely tire, their luck will surely run out, and Garstang will bag a hatful.'

CHAPTER THIRTY-FOUR

The half-time pies were calling and Blakey couldn't resist a chicken Balti pie wrapped in a buttered bap. Geoff opted for crisps. Finley decided on a pint of Fosters.

'Cheer up, lad. It's cup final day,' Blakey said.

Finley closed his eyes. 'Is it too much to ask for a miracle? Just once? In all my life, just one thing, one moment of relief from the stress and the pressure of reality when I need it most ... cos, oh boy, my tomorrow looks as bad as my yesterday, worse probably. Can I just have something ... something to feel good about when I wake up tomorrow in that cold, empty flat? I know it's only a game ... but it's all I've got.'

Blakey had never hugged Finley before, so he didn't put his arms around his old friend, but he wanted to.

'As the players return to the pitch for the second half, I wonder what the Glebe Town manager had to say to his team at half-time. I'm sure he'd have liked to make some changes, but he's got limited options on the bench, so it's as we were as the ref gets things back under way ...'

Oohs and aahs from the fans. More near misses from Garstang FC, more last-ditch defending from Glebe Town. But the performance was better. Less ragged, less scared.

'Before the match, many said that Glebe would just be happy to be here, having failed to make any cup final for decades. But I'm beginning to wonder if they're really here to make up the numbers after all, because they're now playing like a team with nothing to lose. They've enjoyed bright moments in this second half but are yet to have a shot at goal ... One second, we have some breaking news from the touchline. The Glebe Town manager's looking to make his first change of the game, and it looks like Jake Mersey has run his race. He's looked leggy since that knock in the sixty-fifth minute, and the manager must have decided he needs some energy on this right-hand side. So Mersey is making way for number 78, Charlie Campbell.'

Blakey jumped up. 'Bloody hell! I saw him warm up but I didn't think he'd be put on the pitch.'

'Come on, Charlie-Lad!' Finley punched the air. 'Don't forget the shimmy shake. You'll have that lump of a left back on toast.'

The rest of the crowd were unmoved by the substitution. Blakey knew that whenever a player wore a number as high as Charlie's, expectations were limited.

'Seventy-nine minutes played so far and Glebe have defied expectations in this second half, but still the scoreline remains one–nil, and Glebe Town have no route to goal at the moment ... Oh, wait, what's this ...? That's a nice flick from Johnson. It's picked up by Scarper, moved across to Campbell. Campbell's first touch is a good one, he knocks it in front, strides forward and passes his defender, but here comes the centre back. Can Campbell go further? Yes he can! He drops the shoulder and rides the tackle. This is extraordinary ... he's inside the penalty area ... he hits it! Oh! What a goal! It's a match day miracle from out of nowhere! The crowd are on their feet and the stadium is bouncing as nineteen-year-old Charlie Campbell levels the score with an absolute missile from fifteen yards. His shot rifled into the top left-hand corner. The keeper was reaching but

couldn't get anywhere near it. Pick that one out of the net.'

Charlie ran to the crowd and threw himself into the arms of the fans. He was consumed by a mass of arms, hands, and faces red with passion. He turned his back to the cameras and pointed to the name on the back of his shirt. Rachael snapped Blakey's reaction as he screamed and bounced.

'Well, well, well. We have a cup final on our hands all of a sudden. One–one here as play resumes, and how are Garstang going to react? Not well by all accounts, as Johnson dispossesses Edie, passes to Campbell, we've seen this move before ... Campbell's got chalk on his boots now as he taps it beyond Claude and gives chase. He beats Claude in the foot race but here comes Clarke to apprehend ... Oh, but Campbell drops the shoulder and jinks around Clarke, threads it through the legs of Anderson. Only the keeper to beat now! He feints one way, feints the other! He's taken it around the keeper, and ... it's in! It sneaked in at the near post and it's a sensational goal! Two goals in three minutes. Finley John, eat your heart out! The Glebe Town fans are in

dreamland here as Garstang players fall to their knees. Garstang must have thought they had it won. For eighty minutes they had one hand on the trophy, but that young Charlie Campbell turned the game on its head.'

Charlie emerged from under a pile of teammates as the crowd continued to erupt. Blakey's throat hurt from screaming. Geoff punched the air about fifty times, and mania surrounded them as Charlie looked up from the pitch and raised a thumb to the crowd. From the stands, Finley raised one back.

'And who's that Charlie is signalling to in the crowd? Unless my eyes deceive me, it looks like former Glebe Town youth player Finley John, and from here it looks like tears are in the eyes of the old cup hero as Charlie Campbell's moment of magic lights up the stadium.'

CHAPTER THIRTY-FIVE

Finley watched a pan of water on his camping stove. He had set it up a few months ago when they cut off his gas. He was always one step ahead, although he wished he didn't have to be.

It's not true, he thought, a watched pot does boil; it's just really bloody boring.

The door buzzed.

'Whoever now? I've got nothing more you can take, you know, you bastards.' He set the gas to simmer and walked through his empty flat. Cold hung in the air; he could feel it through his coat as he walked through the room. He tried to ignore the outlines in the carpet where his furniture had been. It was still too painful.

He checked the monitor by the door.

'Come in, soft lad.' He pressed the door release and Blakey came ambling in with something under his arm.

'Fancy a cuppa to help with the hangover?' Finley said.

'Aye, why not. Hell of a party that was, eh?'

'Not seen owt like it since 1964. It's the only way to celebrate a result like that. What's that under your arm?'

Blakey put two boxes down on Finley's armchair. Finley instantly recognised them.

'Ella's things … Where the bloody hell did you get those?'

'I met the manager of Capital Re-Allocation Incorporated at the party last night. Turns out, he runs the repo men around here. He's also a big Glebe Town fan, so I swapped him these for a chance to meet Charlie. Sorry I couldn't get the rest of your stuff back, but I thought these would be the most important things.'

Finley turned to the kitchen. 'I best check on the water. It'll have boiled by now.'

'Finley. I think it's time you opened these boxes.'

'Whatever for?'

'I know it's hard, but I think it will help you come to terms with Ella's passing.'

'And why would I want to come to terms with a thing like that?'

The buzzer buzzed again.

'Like Piccadilly Circus in here today.' Finley walked back to the SecurComm unit and saw Geoff grinning cheekily at the camera. He let him in.

'You seen this?' Geoff said, walking in with a fresh copy of the *Glebe Observer*. 'Bloody comedians.'

The headline read: 'The Hip-Replacement Bandits Foil Bank Robbery'.

'Pillocks,' Finley replied. 'We're going to need a new name.'

Blakey rolled his eyes.

Geoff rubbed his chin. 'How about the Baby Boomer Bunch?'

'No, that'll never do,' Finley said.

Geoff clicked a finger. 'I've got it – Geoff's Crew.'

'It's over,' Blakey said. 'We don't need a name.'

Finley's eyes lit up. 'The Boomer Crew!'

'That'll do it,' Geoff said. 'Anyway, there's more to that newspaper so have another look.'

Finley scanned the second story in the top right of the front page.

'Well I never!'

'What's it say?' Blakey said.

'It looks like Derek, I mean *Mr Onions,* has some explaining to do.'

A small picture showed Derek, flanked by police officers, being led towards a police car. Finley read the story aloud: 'High Street bank manager, Derek Onions, 72, is under investigation for allegedly siphoning off 100k from customer accounts. The accusations have arisen after a mandatory internal audit following the recent robbery attempt showed several accounting anomalies.'

'So that's why he hadn't retired!' Blakey said.

'Couldn't have happened to a nicer fella, if you ask me,' Geoff said.

'Too right!' Finley punched the air. 'I'll frame that story and put it on my wall, I will.'

'And here's another thing,' Geoff said, 'turns out Doris was so stunned by the whole episode she forgot we tried to rob the place.'

'Or she didn't believe us in the first place,' Finley said, smiling. 'Ah, that story about Derek has perked me up a bit. I've got some water boiling. Fancy a cuppa? They're used teabags, though.'

'Wait a second,' Geoff said, 'I just need to get something from outside. Be right back.' When he returned, he was out of breath and carrying something large.

'What's that?' Finley said. It looked familiar.

'It's your telly. I fixed it. It was a few dried-out capacitors in the power supply. I've swapped them out, so it's as good as new.' Geoff rested the TV on the armchair. It was a little too heavy for him, and it hit the chair with a bump and knocked Ella's boxes to the floor, spilling their contents across the carpet.

Geoff looked mortified. 'Oh, I am sorry, Finley. I'll pick them up.'

'Forget it. Genie's out of the bottle now. I'll sort it out.' Finley eased himself to his knees and carefully put Ella's things back in the box. Letters, pens, her favourite cigarette lighter, her fanciest brooch, her wedding ring, photographs and a diary. He picked up the diary.

'I'm not sure if I dare read this.' He went to put it in the box but something fell from its pages. He picked up what looked like a slip of paper, read it, and grew short of breath. He walked around the room staring at it.

'What is it?' Blakey said.

'Oh, my god!' He handed it to Blakey. 'Is it me or is this a scratch card? A used scratch card. A bloody winning scratch card!'

'Let's have a look.' Geoff scanned it over Blakey's shoulder. The card's shiny surface gleamed in the daylight and the scratchable part was covered in symbols and numbers.

'Geoff, you double-check it for me,' Blakey said.

Geoff put on his reading glasses. 'Let's see here … match three to win. There's two £1s there. And two £100,000s … no wait, that's three. That's three £100,000s. Wait, what? That means this is a winner. Which means it's worth £100,000!'

He handed the card to Finley. There was no date on it, or an expiry, but on the back was a note written in pen. It read, 'For your future. I love you. Ella xx'.

Finley wiped his eyes with his shirt, but he couldn't stop the heavy, uncontrollable tears from flowing. He thought back to her last days, wondering what he'd do without her, looking at her in the hospital bed, wishing she'd wake up, never knowing that she had one last trick up her sleeve, one last gesture to make sure he'd be okay.

EPILOGUE

A wood pigeon landed on the grass, bobbed and marched, eyes on the prize. He hopped on the tree stump and leapt up to the first floor of the Multiplex Pro bird feeder, a sheltered, multi-tiered seed and suet dispenser complete with birdbath. It was the penthouse apartments of bird feeders. Finley watched from his window and smiled.

The flat was so warm Finley had to remove his coat: no more huddling inside its musty folds all day. He flicked on his new hi-fi as the morning post flopped through the letter box. Mail in hand, Finley hopped into his new power-assisted Comfort Master armchair, noticing a black envelope among the letters. He took a second to admire it. High-quality paper, he thought. Not your average junk mail. But it can't be good news to be sent in such a foreboding colour. Even debt collectors are a bit more upbeat with their choice of stationery.

His phone rang. Blakey.

'Morning,' Finley said.

'You got your post this morning?'

'Yeah.'

'Did you get a black letter?'

Finley checked it over. 'Aye. Looks a bit serious. And there's no address or stamp on it. How'd you know?'

'I got one too. You better open it,' Blakey said.

'I don't think I want to. Who hand-delivers a letter in a sheer black envelope? What is it? A love letter from an undertaker?' Curiosity got the better of him. 'Ah, sod it.' He ripped it open and pulled out a black card marked with white text. The words were all capitalised, shouting.

'An invitation to the Hip-Replacement Bandits,' Finley said. 'Cheeky buggers.'

'It's less of an invitation and more of a demand,' said Blakey.

Finley's phone buzzed like a bee in a bottle. 'Wait a sec. Geoff's trying to get through; let me add him to the call.'

Geoff yelped down the phone, his voice raspy and breathless. 'You got this bloody letter?'

'Morning, Geoff,' Blakey said. 'You got one too?'

Geoff gulped. 'It says that we're requested to attend an urgent meeting with Harry the Hammer at Mr Bigg's Snooker Club on Margate Road. Two p.m. today. Be there or be sorry. I've never heard of a Mr Bigg or a Harry the Hammer before!'

'Me neither,' said Finley.

'I have,' Blakey said, 'but only from urban legends. And from what I've heard, he's not the kind of man you want to keep waiting.'

'What the bloody hell does he want?' Finley said, feeling indignant over the imposition of it all.

'I've no idea, but I think we better go and find out …'

AUTHOR'S NOTE

Thank you for reading *The Boomer Crew*. I'm hoping The Boomer Crew Book 2, *The Joke That Killed*, will be out sometime during late 2023. Feel free to stop by my Facebook page for updates, and please consider leaving a 5-star review on Amazon for this book – it really helps.

ONE LAST THING

If you enjoyed reading *The Boomer Crew,* please consider leaving a review on Amazon to help others find it.

Also, **I hate typos.** This book has been rigorously edited and proofread, but sometimes mistakes do slip through. If you have spotted a typo, please let me know and I'll get it amended.

petereddonbooks@gmail.com

Made in the USA
Coppell, TX
30 September 2023

22235994R00090